The Cry of the Jackal

Other Avalon Books by Michael Sheehan

IN THE SHADOW OF THE BEAR

The CRY of the JACKAL

□

MICHAEL SHEEHAN

AVALON BOOKS
THOMAS BOUREGY AND COMPANY, INC.
401 LAFAYETTE STREET
NEW YORK, NEW YORK 10003

© Copyright 1991 by Michael Sheehan
Library of Congress Catalog Card Number: 91-91950
ISBN 0-8034-8879-3

PRINTED IN THE UNITED STATES OF AMERICA
ON ACID-FREE PAPER
BY HADDON CRAFTSMEN, SCRANTON, PENNSYLVANIA

Once again, to Nancy, with whom life is an adventure

Prologue

The cold March rain tapped politely but insistently on the windows of the large brownstone in an exclusive suburb of Washington, D.C., but no one within paid it any heed. The richly attired men and women, many in formal dress, were too entranced by the string quartet to notice the natural rhythms drumming on the windowpanes.

But two men had been able to tear themselves away from the private performance being given by the world-famous quartet. They sat now, cigars in hand, in a paneled library down the hall from the salon where the performance was taking place. Here, the rhythms of the rain dominated. Even the strong, surging strains of Beethoven stood no chance of wafting through the heavily padded and carefully locked door.

The taller of the two middle-aged men, slender and militarily straight in his tuxedo, rose and walked across the gleaming oak floor to a nearby sideboard to replenish their snifters with cognac. He replaced the bulbous crystal stopper on the Waterford decanter and carried both snifters back to the marble fireplace, cradling them in his

1

palms. He handed a snifter to his guest with a slight nod
of the head and then sat down in one of the leather chairs
that flanked the glowing fireplace. He took an apprecia-
tive sip of the cognac, carefully set it down on the glass-
topped table between them, and looked expectantly at the
other man.

"So, what do you have for me?" he asked.

The other man uncrossed his legs and shifted in his
chair. He did not look quite as elegant in his dark-gray
suit and rep tie, and he carried a few pounds too many
for his own good, but he, too, exuded an air of quiet
authority. "As usual, I have both good news and bad."

"Let's have the bad news."

The guest smiled. This was so characteristic of the
Director's style. Deal with the problems first. Then, if
there is any time or energy left, indulge in the good news.
A case of self-discipline carried out to the nth degree.
Not that he was complaining—this trait had served the
Agency and the country well.

"The bad news is that a mole has infiltrated our Ethiopian theater. We can't tell where yet. We've monitored
some messages that the other side—more precisely, the
Cubans—shouldn't have. I don't need to tell you that
this could seriously compromise Operation Thunder-
bolt."

The Director took another sip of cognac. Covertly aid-
ing the rebels who had been chafing under a Marxist
regime for the last two decades was even more compli-
cated now than in the past. In these days of *glasnost*, no
one was more embarrassed by the doctrinaire rulers of
Ethiopia than the Russians. He knew for a fact that Mos-

cow was trying its best to tone down the true believers and bring them into line with post-Cold War realities.

But the Russian shift in Ethiopian policy had to take place behind the scenes until their Supreme Soviet decided what to do about the Cuban presence in Ethiopia. Castro was already furious over what he considered the betrayal of the spirit of the 1917 revolution, and positive proof that the Russians were winking at an increasing American role in overthrowing a Marxist regime might lead to a very messy and a very public confrontation. Five years ago, an American administration would have jumped at the chance to see a Russian leader in trouble. Now it went out of its way to protect him.

The Director caught himself tapping on the arm of his chair in time to the drumming of the rain on the window. He reached for his snifter and looked at his first assistant. "What course of action does the Council recommend?"

"Send in a specialist, of course. Someone who can check out operations and loyalty. Someone who can plug a leak."

The Director smiled wryly. "Donald, you didn't have to come here to tell me that. What's really on your mind?"

The first assistant acknowledged this without surprise or guilt. Each man knew the other like the back of his own hand. "You're right. What I'm agonizing over is the specialist. Not just anyone will do, of course, but we've got a decent-enough pool. Naturally, I'd like to send the best of the lot, but there's a problem."

The Director watched him attentively. About the only flaw that his first assistant ever exhibited was a bit too much conscience. But then some people would see that as a virtue. "What problem?" he asked.

"The best agent available is Brent Collins."

The Director leaned back against his chair, searching his mental files. "Collins . . . Collins. The name sounds familiar, but you're going to have to refresh my memory." He raised his hand. "No—wait. Isn't he the young agent who was almost terminated last year? Colombia, wasn't it?"

The first assistant shook his head in admiration at the Director's memory. "Exactly. He was caught in an ambush near Medellin. We just about lost him."

"Are you saying that he's not quite physically ready for the assignment? Well, there's no way I'd be willing to compromise on that. You know the rules, Donald. We'll always take care of our own—a temporary desk job or a research position, perhaps—but field agents must be at total capacity."

The first assistant nodded emphatically. "No, I'm not about to change the rules, either. He's physically ready, all right. In fact, he's amazed everybody by his rate of recovery. He's been approved by the Agency medical board, and you know how picky they are. But the problem isn't physical."

The Director sighed in understanding. Collins must have suffered an agent's worst nightmare—a crisis of nerve. He scrutinized the man sitting next to him. Donald wouldn't compromise on that score any more than he would compromise on an agent's physical condition. So either the psychological profiles were ambiguous or there was a more personal element here. He raised an eyebrow, inviting Donald to continue.

"I know what you're thinking. But he passed the psychological board too. No, the problem is Keller."

The Director nodded. Keller was legendary head of the survival-training program. Every agent dreaded the required annual refresher course, but every live agent had reason to sing its praises.

"Keller has a sixth sense about these things. He's pushed and he's prodded and nothing has cracked, but he tells me that he's uneasy about Collins. Nothing that he can put his finger on, though, and so he's not ready to scrub him. He admits that Collins is probably the best agent on our current roster, but he thinks he just may hear the subtle tick of a time bomb. He suspects that Collins may be carrying something more than physical scars away from Medellin. If so, it eluded the shrinks."

"If there's an element of doubt, why not just bypass Collins and assign someone else? What makes him so indispensable for this assignment?"

"You've put your finger on it. I'm not wed to the word 'indispensable,' mind you, but he's got a unique qualification. The leader of the largest and the most reliable rebel group that we're backing in Ethiopia is named Taamrat Karkar. And it just so happens that he and Brent Collins were college roommates at Georgetown."

The Director laced his fingers together in front of his chest. "I see," he said. "We do have a bit of a dilemma, don't we? Why don't you get the cognac this time?"

Chapter One

Brent Collins looked unobtrusively around the bustling Aden airport terminal. All about him, men and women in business suits, flowing Mideastern robes, and in other national costumes, rubbed shoulders in a colorful and cosmopolitan display. It was Brent's first trip to the People's Democratic Republic of Yemen, which was only a hop, skip, and jump from the African continent, but he was looking for a specific face. That face, which belonged to a fellow agent, was also supposed to be looking for him.

Ten minutes past the assignation time, Brent decided to wait in the coffee shop. He had eaten on the flight over, but the central location of the coffee shop would give him a good observation point while getting him out of the heavy flow of foot traffic. Brent slid onto a stool that gave him an unobstructed view of the terminal through the plate-glass divider, and then he planted his briefcase firmly on his lap. But before he could get the waitress's attention, he heard himself being paged over the PA system:

7

"Mr. Collins. Mr. Brent Collins. Please report to the service desk at the Yemen Airways ticket counter."

Brent slid off the stool just as the waitress walked toward him with a menu in her hand. He smiled and shrugged, pointing to the speaker overhead, and headed back into the main part of the terminal. At the ticket counter, he identified himself to the uniformed young woman: "I'm Collins—Brent Collins. I was just paged."

"Oh, yes, Mr. Collins, there is a call for you." She slid a red phone across the counter for his convenience. He frowned as he placed his briefcase on the counter and picked up the receiver. Obviously, there was going to be a delay, and he was on a rather tight schedule. The other agent should have known that.

"Yes. This is Brent Collins. Hello?"

Silence. There was no response. The hairs on the back of Brent's neck rose in warning. He had just been suckered by one of the oldest tricks in the book. He had identified himself to a pair of watching eyes by answering the page and picking up the phone.

He replaced the receiver and casually pushed the phone back across the counter. The ticket agent was occupied with another customer and hadn't noticed the lack of dialogue. He picked up his briefcase and turned away from the counter. He let his eyes sweep quickly but thoroughly around the area.

To his right, about twenty yards away, a tall man with poor posture and a pencil-thin mustache was assiduously cleaning his fingernails with a file. Brent caught him looking. Count one. Straight ahead, next to an arrangement of contoured lounge seats near the coffee shop, a man in a colorful dashiki stood by himself, carefully watching the man with the nail file. Count two. And to the left, stepping out of a telephone kiosk and staring unabashedly at Brent, was a muscular man with a shaved head. Count three.

Slowly, the three mismatched men began to converge on Brent. He knew that they were coming for him, and they knew that he knew. To Brent, that showed the measure either of their determination or of their foolhardiness. Either way, they spelled trouble.

Without any warning, and moving quite casually, Brent stepped over the baggage scale and behind the counter. Before the startled ticket agent could tell him that he belonged on the other side, Brent stooped and crawled through the flaps of material that led to the baggage conveyor belt behind the wall. He found himself wedged between a large brown suitcase and a blue duffel bag. Behind him, he could hear a hubbub of reaction.

He rode the conveyor belt for about ten feet, critically surveying the area in which he found himself. He was being carried past a whole series of industrial-strength wire-mesh shelves that extended from the floor to the ceiling and were set at right angles to the conveyor belt. On the shelves sat luggage and packages of all sizes and varieties. Either this was a baggage and freight storage area for upcoming flights or it was a very large lost-and-found department. As he came even with yet another aisle, Brent stepped off the belt and darted between the shelves. Coming to the cross aisle, he ducked behind the end of a shelf, unlocked his briefcase, and extracted a pistol with a silencer. He gave thanks for the sanctity of his diplomatic pouch as he slid the clasp back in place. Behind him, the babble of shouts and warnings continued from the area of the ticket counter. He set down the briefcase on the floor and waited patiently.

Within seconds, the large muscular man, crouched on hands and knees between a footlocker and a cardboard box, moved past Brent's line of sight on the conveyor belt like a duck in a shooting gallery. Suddenly sensing Brent's eyes boring into him, the man turned and raised his arm in Brent's direction. Before the man could fire, the pistol in Brent's hand coughed quietly and recoiled against his palm. Instantly, the shaved head bowed down and touched the conveyor belt as if paying homage to the gods of aviation.

Brent waited patiently. For the next few seconds, the conveyor belt carried nothing but standard baggage. Just about the time that he got the picture, he sensed movement behind him. As he ducked his head and dropped to the left, a burst of pain shot through his right shoulder, driving the wind from his lungs and forcing him to release his grasp on the pistol. As it clattered to the floor and slid away out of reach, he rolled over on his back and raised his left arm defensively.

Brent pulled his arm back just in time to keep it from being shattered by another explosive kick directed at him by the man in the dashiki. Taking advantage of the man's thrusting forward motion as he pivoted on his left foot to deliver the blow with his right, Brent hooked the man's left ankle with the tip of his shoe and upended him. Off balance and unable to recover, the man cracked his head loudly against the sharp edge of the metal shelf support and then slumped to the ground. Brent jumped up and watched him warily, but the man did not raise his head from the widening pool of blood under him.

One to go now. Brent bent over to pick up the pistol from the floor, and the action unwittingly saved his life. As he reached for the butt of the gun, a knife zipped over his head, clattered noisily against the metal shelf in front of him, and fell uselessly to the tile floor. Brent whirled and aimed the pistol barrel just above the pencil-thin mustache. The man froze, his right arm still extended in front of him, silently conceding Brent's advantage.

Brent advanced cautiously, arms extended straight in front of him, weapon unwavering in his hands. When he was about three feet away, he stopped and barked out, "Turn around! Place your open hands against the shelf! Step back and spread your feet!"

Whether from long practice or from the clarity of Brent's instructions, the man complied instantly. Brent moved in closer and kicked against the insides of the man's shoes to widen his stance. Then he patted him down carefully. After extracting one knife from behind the man's belt and another from his left sock, he dropped them to the floor and then kicked them backward out of reach.

Brent took a quick glance behind him. He had to retrieve his briefcase from the floor before leaving the baggage area to hand this man over. "Put your hands behind your neck—both hands! Now follow me slowly! Keep the same distance! No sudden moves!"

Brent began to move backward toward the briefcase, the barrel of his pistol locked on the man's chest. His prisoner did as instructed, his normally hunched shoulders now even more bent in defeat. He looked utterly pathetic.

Then, as Brent moved carefully backward, he stepped on one of the knives. He looked down quickly to kick it back even more. In that split second, the man made a move. He dug at his ear with his finger, extracted a small capsule, and jammed it into his mouth. Brent lunged for his arm but was too late. Even as his fingers closed around the man's bony wrist, he heard the crunch of teeth and saw the utter despair written in those moist eyes. Suddenly the air smelled of bitter almonds, and Brent watched helplessly as the man fell to the floor in convulsions.

Brent looked down at the man's rigid body. Cyanide was not a pretty way to go, but, then, neither was a knife between the shoulder blades. Brent retrieved his briefcase, stowed the pistol, and snapped the lock in place. Just what other surprises was this mission going to bring?

The twin-hulled assault boat skipped over the top of the moonlit waters of the Red Sea. Thumping rhythmically, it sliced segments out of the evenly spaced waves created by passing supertankers. Standing in the bow, Brent scanned the watery path ahead through the infrared scope attached to his helmet. Occasionally, he felt himself begin to topple as the craft slammed into a deeper trough, but each time he was steadied by the safety harness that linked him to the throbbing hull.

Brent was pumped with nervous energy. The first half of his new assignment was officially underway. A three-man commando team was escorting him from their mother ship, a nuclear submarine that patrolled the troubled Mideast and the northern coast of Africa. Their nighttime foray into the coastal waters off Ethiopia had so far been undetected and without incident, and Brent wanted it to remain that way. After the incident yesterday in the Aden airport, he could do without more welcoming parties.

He was looking forward to his meeting with Taamrat, both personally and professionally. Although they had never lost touch after their college days, they had not had a chance to see each other for the past three years. He smiled as he recalled some of their pranks back at school.

A small-town boy fortunate enough to earn a scholarship to a school his family couldn't have afforded, Brent had been painfully shy, and he might have spent his college days observing life instead of living it. But on the first day of freshman orientation week, Taamrat and his boundless energy had come bursting into their dorm room and into Brent's life, and neither man had been the same again.

Taamrat seized life with both hands. The somewhat spoiled son of an Ethiopian diplomat, Taamrat had had enough self-confidence and cosmopolitan sophistication for the both of them. His dynamic example opened Brent to possibilities within himself that he hadn't known existed. And from Brent, Taamrat had learned something about stability and responsibility. Under Brent's unassuming tutelage, he began to pay more attention to the intellectual qualities within him that his playboy existence had undervalued. And so the unlikely pair became steadfast friends.

Brent's reverie was interrupted by a voice coming at him in stereo on his helmet headset:

"Fishing vessel dead ahead, sir. Running-light configurations match the prearranged code."

Quickly, Brent applied his eye to the padded viewfinder. He was slightly chagrined at having indulged in woolgathering. "I confirm that, Lieutenant," he said. He flexed his fingers and rubbed his chilled hands together. This was it—the secret offshore meeting was about to take place. He braced himself as the crew of the assault boat, weapons in firing position, engaged in a precautionary sweep around the fishing vessel. Then they cut the engines and the boat drifted in for boarding.

He retrieved his briefcase from the waterproof locker. From the professional point of view, this assignment represented an entirely new level for Brent. It involved elements of diplomacy and of subtle government dealings to which he had not been privy in any of his previous assignments. He recognized it as a crucial step up the career ladder. He smiled as he placed his foot on the rope ladder thrown down from above.

A familiar face was waiting for him at the top.

"Hey, Big B! Give me five—if you can still count that high!"

"Yo, Little T! When are you going to stop taking them ugly pills?" Brent pulled back from their vigorous bear hug and studied his old roommate at arm's length. From the halo of tight, black curls to the almost-tailored cut of his fatigues, Taamrat still looked like a movie star. The only discernible changes were the faint lines crinkling the dark bronze skin around his eyes and mouth. But given the high-pressure life that Taamrat now led, Brent figured that his friend was entitled to some stress lines.

Taamrat slapped him on the arm. "Good to see you, man. How's the spy business treating you these days? Overthrown any interesting countries lately? Or have the Russian brothers been teaching you about cooperation?"

"Watch it, Rambo. You're the one who's in battle dress, not me."

"Yeah, you always did have trouble finding a good tailor, didn't you?" He flicked some imaginary lint off Brent's black woolen sweater. "Those off-the-rack rags just don't do anything for you, man. I keep telling you— discount don't count." He draped his arm round Brent's shoulders. "Come on, let's go below deck. We've got some catching up to do."

Later, when their personal odysseys had been recounted and old lies had been hooted down, they turned to business. Taamrat's business was revolution, something that always interested the Agency. Headquartered in the province of Eritrea, Taamrat had spent the last two years engaging in intense guerrilla warfare, seeking to overthrow the unwelcome official regime. In that short time, his tenacity and ferocity had won him a loyal, if not well-equipped, following. Most interesting to Washington was the fact that he had shown considerable talent at uniting rival rebel factions, something that no one had been able to do before.

"What you've got to understand about my people is that this has little to do with pure ideology. We're not about to die for somebody else's ism. These are turf wars. I mean, I lived in the States for years and I loved every second of it, but I'm telling you that there's feudal blood coursing through my veins. I can live under just about any form of government, but don't go messing with my traditions or with my land. That I *will* die for!"

Taamrat went on to make an impassioned plea for more U.S. involvement in the form of humanitarian aid and military supplies. Brent had been expecting such a request, and for the purposes of this mission, he had been authorized on the highest authority to assure Taamrat that both kinds of help would be forthcoming. He seized the opportunity gladly, and told his friend:

"Okay, here's the scoop. Next month, a joint committee will introduce a bipartisan bill in Congress, and after a lot of patriotic speeches and posturing for C-Span, the bill will pass. Your country is going to get a very significant increase in food and medical supplies. But there's a catch—some members of Congress are going to demand assurances about the distribution network. They're steamed because of the government pilfering of donated supplies that's gone on in the past. They're going to want an ironclad guarantee that ordinary Ethiopian citizens will get the supplies, not some corrupt quartermasters."

"They don't want that any more than I do, Brent."

"I'm sure. That's one of the things I'm here to talk about. We figure that you'll have some ideas on how to keep the wolves honest. I know that you're not part of the official government. . . ."

"Not yet, you mean."

"Not part of the government *yet,* but if you'll give us the names of officials or agencies that you trust, we'll make sure that their names get worked into the small print of the bill."

"I just love your democracy in action."

"Beats the pants off tyranny any day, dude." Brent leaned forward on his bench. "And as for the military aid, here's how that pitch will slide. Within the very near future, you'll be contacted by a representative of a certain Mideast country, soon to be named. That rep will make you an offer you can't refuse. We're talking arms, portable missiles, and personnel carriers. Oh, and some military advisers.'' He paused for effect. ''You won't be billed for the shipment. An uncle of yours is going to pay for it. Under the table, of course.''

Taamrat broke into a wide smile. ''Pay it again, Sam?''

''You got it. That's the uncle. But to make this work, I've got to go back with proof that your efforts at consolidating those splintered guerrilla forces have been successful. My people need to be certain that they're dealing with someone who can deliver.'' Brent looked at his friend apologetically. ''If it were just up to me, T, there'd be no conditions. You know that.''

Taamrat took a deep breath. This was a crucial moment for him. ''I understand. But it's a legitimate concern for your side. It's what old Professor Copi would have called a quid pro quo, a trade-off. So let me tell you what I've been doing about creating a united front.''

Long into the night, they traded information, hammered out details and conditions, and set up provisional codes and contacts. They would be meeting again, of course, but Brent made it clear that he needed substantial material right away to begin to uncap the aid pipelines.

During the course of their negotiations, Brent brought up the other big item on his agenda: ''T, we've got a real serious security problem. Someone in the know is feeding the other side information that we don't want them to have. We don't know where the leak is yet, but it could turn out to be big enough to sink your revolution if it's not plugged. If it's one of our people, we'll find it and seal it. But I want you to be careful. And I'm going to ask you to run a security check on your own people, and

I mean everybody, even your closest advisers. That's a door that we can't enter.''

Surprisingly, Taamrat took some offense. At first he insisted heatedly that his people were incapable of turning on their own. They were warriors bound by a blood oath. He was adamant that the Agency and the Agency alone must be the source of the leak. It was only after Brent pointed out, rather forcefully, that the leaders of the current, hated regime were fellow Ethiopians, not imports from America, that Taamrat began to relent. By the end of their meeting, they were again the best of friends and political allies.

Though his business with Taamrat was far from finished, Brent was now about to enter the second phase of his twofold mission, a security check on Agency personnel and operations. As soon as the submarine slipped back through the strait into the Gulf of Aden, he would return to Yemen and come above ground again, both literally and in terms of profile. A business flight from the airport at Aden was scheduled to depart this afternoon; he had been booked on that flight. In practically no time at all, he would be arriving in Addis Ababa, the capital of Ethiopia.

Addis Ababa assaulted Brent's senses like few other cities on earth. His nostrils were assailed by the odors of exotic foods, pungent spices, gamy livestock, and putrid sewage. His eyes were attracted by constant swirls of motion, kaleidoscopic flashes of color, and an impossible juxtaposition of ancient and modern. And his ears were bombarded by the strident cries of merchants, the shrill urgency of beggars, and the unbearable din of grinding gears, blaring horns, and bleating pack animals. It was tempting to stand on a corner and simply give himself up to the experience, but he had an appointment to keep.

Figure by figure, he compared the Arabic address on the small card in his hand with the address crudely painted on the dirty plate-glass window before him. It certainly didn't look like an appropriate site for a translation service. Like many of the buildings in this particular neighborhood, the frame structure had seen better days. Patches of a once-bright blue paint clung to its surface here and there, but for the most part, the paint had long ago succumbed to gritty wind and baking weather.

A flapping sound overhead caught his attention, and looking up, he saw a clothesline dancing with colorful garments. The line was attached to a pulley right under a fourth-floor window. His gaze idly followed its length as it extended high over the narrow lane and ended at a fourth-floor window across the way. He mused about the arrangement. What do the neighbors in the facing buildings do—hang clothes on alternate days of the week? Or do they have an early-morning scramble to see who gets to use the line for that day? The arrangement spoke both of neighborly cooperation and the potential for bitter conflict.

He checked the address again, then returned the card to his wallet. A small group of curious children had gathered around this tall foreigner, and at the sight of his wallet, a great jostling and shouting for attention ensued. He didn't know the language they spoke, but there was no doubt about the language of their outstretched palms, and he looked sadly at them. He had read that some of these young beggars could make more from foreign tourists in one day than their fathers could earn in one month. Inadvertently, softhearted tourists were contributing to the breakdown of families by robbing parents of their rightful economic role. But listening to his heart instead of his head, he distributed some money and stepped quickly into the first-floor shop.

It was cooler in here, and even darker than the shadowy street he had just left. It took a few moments for his eyes to adjust. He looked around. This did not look like one of the city's more successful stores. Half the dusty shelves were empty; the others had gaping spaces between the merchandise. And it was impossible to tell what kind of a store it was. Some shelves held cans—vegetables or fruit, according to the pictures on the faded labels. One shelf had bolts of saffron-colored muslin cloth, but the one below it supported open cardboard boxes of nails and screws. Some of the nails, Brent noticed, were bent.

A movement from the right side of the room caught Brent's eye. Through a curtain of beads hanging down over a low doorway, there emerged one of the fattest men that Brent had ever seen. The man must have weighed at least four hundred pounds. He was wrapped in a striped garment that made him look like a walking circus tent. He waddled his way ponderously behind a wooden counter, wheezing with every step. And most curious of all, he was not Ethiopian but European.

The man's rubbery lips parted in greeting: "*Bon jour, monsieur.*" His voice rumbled across the counter, a deep, hollow sound that reminded Brent of a foghorn.

Brent spoke slowly and distinctly. "Good day. I wonder if you could help me. I'm looking for the translation services of Linguists Limited—for a Mr. Chelga, to be exact.''

Brent could have sworn that there was a flash of sudden interest in the man's eyes at the mention of the name Chelga. Then his heavy lids dropped even more, concealing any thoughts that he might be having. An oppressive silence ensued. Brent was about to repeat his request in rusty high-school French when the man pointed above his head with a sausagelike finger. ''Upstairs, next floor,'' he said.

Brent looked around. There was no staircase in sight. He shrugged to communicate confusion. The man's porcine eyes held Brent's for a moment. It was impossible to read exactly what lurked behind them, but the man seemed both wary and sinister at the same time.

The man's gigantic head swiveled ponderously to his right. ''Outside,'' he said. ''Another door. Then up.'' His lips clamped shut with finality. Brent felt dismissed. He had the distinct feeling that this merchant didn't want him in his store even if he proposed to buy everything in sight. Very curious.

After nodding his thanks, Brent turned and walked back outside. The children were gone and the lane was now totally deserted. *Probably siesta time*, Brent thought. *Or whatever the Ethiopian equivalent is.* He spotted the door to which the merchant had referred, but there was still no sign for a translation service. He surmised that they must be working on the barest of budgets.

Brent swung the door open and poked his head into the hallway. A rickety staircase without benefit of banisters ascended to a dark landing above. It wasn't very inviting, but this had to be it. He left the door open to provide some light and began the trek upward.

Halfway up the stairs, he heard a door slamming in the distance above. Light, rapid footsteps followed—it seemed on another staircase—and then a woman appeared at the top of the stairs and began to descend. She was young and pretty. Her bronze-colored skin was accentuated by the red wraparound garment she wore. As Brent turned sideways to allow her to pass, he greeted her cheerfully. Eyes downcast, she slid by without a murmur and was out the door almost before he knew it. Brent addressed the empty staircase below him: "Was it something I said?" His words echoed back to him faintly. With a shrug, he continued up the stairs.

The landing presented him with two choices. To his left was an archway framing another wooden stairway up to the next floor. That must be where the young woman had come from. And straight ahead was a glass-paneled door. The murky light coming through its frosted panes accentuated the dust that rose lazily from the floor and floated around the narrow hallway. Brent walked to the door where *Linguists Limited* was stenciled neatly in block letters on the top panel of glass. Underneath it was something written in Arabic. He knocked lightly on the door and entered without waiting for a response.

He found himself in a drab office. A battered desk with an armless swivel chair behind it, two straight-backed chairs for visitors, a dark green four-drawer file cabinet, and a few old dictionaries on a small bookshelf—that was it. Standing by an open file-cabinet drawer, with his back to Brent, was a man in a wrinkled brown suit.

He turned, smiled, and extended his hand as he walked

toward Brent. "Ah! You must be Mr. Collins, to whom I spoke on the telephone. I am Mr. Chelga, at your service. I have been expecting you." Brent shook hands and took a straight-backed chair, as directed. Mr. Chelga was about fifty years old. His short-cropped black hair showed flecks of white here and there. As he plopped down in the squeaky swivel chair behind the desk, his open suit coat revealed a substantial paunch that extended over his belt.

Dangerously out of shape, Brent observed disapprovingly, but then suspended his judgment. It wasn't fair to apply professional standards to Chelga. After all, he was simply a stringer, not a full-time agent. The Agency employed countless such men and women all over the world. Their job was to keep their eyes and ears open for useful information as they pursued otherwise normal, often drab, lives. Their involvement with the Agency was marginal and strictly limited, and their motivation ranged from simple greed to the highest ideological principles.

Brent began his probe: "Mr. Chelga, I'm new to this country and could use your help. Could you tell me about your operations here?"

Chelga beamed at the chance. "First of all, welcome to my country. It is not without its troubles, but it is beautiful, is it not?"

Brent opened his mouth to answer, but Chelga swept on before he could respond. The man seemed to be hungry for an audience.

"My operations, yes. I run a first-class service here. First class. I hope this does not sound immodest, but there you are. Translations of legal documents, foreign business invoices, letters from abroad. Expert tutoring in many languages. Writing letters in their own language for the sadly illiterate, of whom there are many, alas. All first-class services.''

Brent interrupted Chelga as the man paused to take a breath: ''I can certainly see that you run a class act here, Mr. Chelga, but I was referring more to your special services for my company.''

''A class act.'' Chelga smiled in delight as he savored the phrase. ''This is a new idiom to me. A class act. Very good.'' He leaned forward confidentially and lowered his voice. ''Now as to your company, as you say, I am happy to serve it in my own humble way.'' He assumed what was intended to be a modest expression. ''Certain inconsequential documents that I translate, certain small matters that come to my attention—these I pass on in the interests of international cooperation.''

Brent caught the thinly disguised trace of self-importance and decided to feed it. ''You are too modest, Mr. Chelga. I can assure you that your work is highly appreciated.''

Chelga spread his hands in a gesture of demure thanks. ''It is most unfortunate that your wonderful country is not in favor with my government in these troubled times. But this does not mean that all of my countrymen have lost their memories.'' He lowered his voice again. ''Let me assure you that many of us have not forgotten the great respect your country showed to our beloved emperor, Haile Selassie. Though he is with his grieving children no more, the current state of affairs will not last forever.'' He waggled his finger emphatically. ''No, indeed.''

''Well, we appreciate that, believe me.'' Brent was

inclined to assign Chelga to the fuzzy ideologue category. He seemed to be an unrepentant monarchist, a rather unpopular thing to be in a Marxist society. As a source of information, he was small potatoes and a bit amateurish, perhaps, but probably committed for reasons other than the money alone. Obviously, a desire to feel important also played a large role. At any rate, Brent doubted that Chelga knew anything about the Agency and its network beyond the name of his immediate contact. Still, he had better check.

"Mr. Chelga, would you mind confirming for me the name of your contact?"

For the first time during the interview, Brent saw a hint of fear in Chelga's eyes. What was that all about? He thought for a moment. Of course. It probably sounded as if Brent didn't have the slightest idea who the contact was. From Chelga's point of view, that would throw understandable suspicion on the purpose of Brent's visit and on his very identity.

"I'm sorry," Brent added. "I may have phrased that poorly. For security reasons, I need to confirm certain things about operations here. With your considerable experience, I'm sure that you can understand that. Here. . . ." Brent reached into an inner jacket pocket and extracted a notebook and a pen. Using his crossed leg to shield what he was writing, he scribbled a name on a fresh sheet and then tore it out. Folding it in half and then into quarters, he placed the paper on the desk between them. "That is the name of your contact. First tell me who it is, and then look at what I've written. That way, we will both be satisfied."

Chelga looked cautiously at Brent and then at the folded

piece of paper. He seemed to relax. Then he nodded. "Yes. This is a good way. For both of us." He placed his hand protectively over the paper and looked at Brent. "His name is Paul Grober. He is the assistant chargé d'affaires in the Swiss embassy." Chelga unfolded the paper quickly and looked at the name that Brent had written. He smiled in relief and waved the paper happily. "As you already know."

Brent nodded. "Exactly. I hope that you haven't taken this personally. You do understand that this is merely procedure."

Chelga dismissed any offense with a gracious wave of his hand. "No, no, I assure you that I understand perfectly. It is wise to be discreet." He leaned forward and winked conspiratorially. "In fact, if you will forgive me for my deception, that is why I did not mention my backup contact." He chuckled proudly and began to tear the notebook paper into tiny scraps.

Brent looked at him blankly. What on earth was he talking about? For obvious reasons, the Agency never gave stringers more than one contact name. To keep a low profile, it simply didn't assign backup contacts to stringers. If the Agency needed to, it could always find a way to contact the stringers. But it wasn't about to give out gratuitous information. "Your backup?" he asked casually.

"Yes, of course. My other contact is Dr. Carlson. As you already know."

Brent felt a sinking sensation. Something was radically wrong here. "Do you have a first name on this Dr. Carlson?"

Chelga looked at Brent quizzically. Then he chuckled.

"Oh, Mr. Collins. You are by nature cautious, are you not? This is very good. No, I do not know the first name. I have never met this Dr. Carlson. It is merely a surname to me. But you will give me the first name, no?"

Brent decided to take Chelga into his confidence. This piece of disinformation could become a serious source of danger to him. "I must tell you something. There is no Dr. Carlson in our agency."

"I beg your pardon?"

"Dr. Carlson is not one of us. I never heard of a Dr. Carlson in this field of operation. Where did you get this information?"

Chelga looked confused. "No Dr. Carlson? But surely. . . ."

"Please, Mr. Chelga, I've got to know. Where did you get Dr. Carlson's name? Was it from Gruber?" Brent certainly hoped not, but it wouldn't be the first time that a surrogate had gone wrong. Depending on other embassies to gather your information had its problems, but when a country like Ethiopia cut off diplomatic ties with the United States, there was no alternative.

"Gruber? No. He does not give me information. *I* give information to *him*." Chelga waved a hand impatiently. "No, no. This information was from Etienne."

Brent's head began to swim. This was getting worse every second. "And who is Etienne?"

Chelga slapped his forehead in annoyance at himself. "Of course! So sorry. You are new here, as you said. You do not know Etienne. He is a member of the French FBI."

"The *French* FBI?"

"Yes, yes. Every nation, it seems, is represented in

my country in a secret way. Very fertile for information."
He misinterpreted Brent's expression. "No, no—that is
all right. Do not feel bad. We take no offense. We understand the need for intelligence, as you Americans
say."

"How do you know that this Etienne is a member of
the . . . French FBI?" Brent almost stumbled over the lu-
dicrous title.

"Oh, well, I have some small skills in discovering
things, as you know. You have acknowledged this."
Chelga sounded almost reproachful.

"You mean he told you so?"

Chelga shrugged uncomfortably. "Well, nothing so
direct, you understand. But one is able to put one piece
here and one piece there."

Brent decided to be blunt. Chelga's feelings were no
longer paramount. "Did you tell Etienne about your work
for us?"

Chelga stiffened as if he had been slapped in the face.
He looked at Brent disdainfully. "Only a man who does
not know me could make this suggestion. No, sir, I assure
you that I did not." He looked down studiously at the
small strips of notebook paper in his palm. "If you will
excuse me for a moment, I will now dispose of this
message." He looked at Brent challengingly. "As a good
soldier always does." He arose, walked across the room
with exaggerated dignity, and disappeared through a
doorway.

Brent heard a flushing sound and the clatter of a lid
being slammed down. He had certainly ruffled Chelga's
feathers. He was sorry about that. But he had little doubt

that Chelga would be easy prey for someone who knew the power of flattery.

Brent grunted as a disturbing thought occurred to him. The mysterious agent called himself Etienne and supposedly worked for France. And the huge shopkeeper downstairs had greeted Brent in French. Too many coincidences. Etienne was probably the name of the shopkeeper.

Brent was about to call out an urgent question to Chelga when he felt the slightest trace of a breeze on the back of his neck. Before he could turn around, he was unconscious.

Chapter Two

Brent awoke to the sound of someone coughing. *That's what smoking will do to your lungs*, he thought woozily. *You should have read the Surgeon General's warning.* The coughing grew louder. It seemed to be quite close to Brent's ear. Then it dawned on him: *He* was the one who was coughing.

Funny, he thought, *I don't even smoke.* Smoke! His eyes snapped open and he was instantly wary. He was lying on the right side of his face. An ant was crawling across the dusty wooden floor about three inches away from his nose. It was ambitiously carrying a huge crumb on its back. Brent's head was throbbing and he felt nauseated. More disturbing, the room was filled with dense smoke.

He coughed again and sat up slowly, trying not to move his aching head too quickly. He reached around with his left hand and gingerly felt the back of his head. There was a huge welt there. No wonder his head hurt. He brought his hand back and rubbed his eyes. They were stinging and full of tears. He had to get away from all this smoke.

He felt a jolt of adrenaline. Fire! The building was on fire! Forgetting the pain in his head, he jumped to his feet. There was no sign of Chelga. There was just an empty room quickly filling with intolerable smoke.

He stumbled to the bathroom door. It was closed. He turned the knob and tried to push the door open. Something was blocking the way. Leaning heavily against the door with his shoulder, he managed to shove it forward just a few inches. Applying his eye to the narrow opening, he saw Chelga sprawled on the bloody tile floor. One look at his eternally puzzled face told Brent that Chelga would never succumb to flattery again.

Brent turned wearily away from the bathroom door and shuffled to the window. It was stuck. He tugged vigorously at the sash handles. Then, through the filthy glass, he caught sight of the metal bars crisscrossing the outside of the window. He dropped his arms. Even if he managed to get it open, there would be no escape through this window.

He moved toward the office door. Smoke was billowing under it from the hallway outside. He touched the doorknob carefully. It was cool to the touch. It would be all right to open the door. He turned the knob and pulled, but all that he got was resistance and the rattle of a lock.

This was no time for socially correct behavior, and he picked up one of the straight-backed chairs and hurled it through the lower frosted glass panel in the door. Large wisps of smoke pursued the chair through the breaking glass and out into the hallway and then even larger billows began to pour back into the room from the hallway through the now gaping hole.

Brent kicked and scraped the remaining splinters of

glass from their frame with his right shoe. Then he squeezed through the gap and pushed his way through the smoke to the top of the landing. There he was hit by a wall of heat. In an instant, perspiration covered his brow. The temperature at the top of the stairs was incredible, and his skin felt as if it were being roasted. He raised his hand to shield his face. Through the sea of smoke that made the staircase impenetrable, he could see red and yellow balls of flame surging up toward him.

His chest heaved now as he tried to get a clear breath. Smoke and heat were making it impossible to breathe. He fell back as a sheet of flame suddenly thrust itself up the staircase and blackened the wall inches from his face. He could smell his hair and eyebrows beginning to singe. Almost in a panic, he looked around for a way out.

The staircase up to the next floor! He couldn't see it because of the rolling waves of smoke, but he had to be within a few feet of it. He dropped to his knees and groped along the edge of the wall. Reaching the archway, he edged himself sideways until his hand made contact with the first stair up. His brain told him that to go up was to be trapped. But his body told him that any alternative was better than this searing, breath-stealing heat. He began a desperate scramble up the steep stairs.

After three steps there was a small landing, and then the staircase made a sharp turn to the right. Hugging the wall, he continued to stumble upward, each inhale of breath deeply painful, and each exhale ending in a spasm of coughing. There was another sharp turn to the right. A few more steps, and then he pitched forward and fell to his hands and knees. He had run out of stairs; he had reached the third-floor landing.

Here the smoke was slightly less dense than on the floor below, but it was still thick enough to obscure visibility seriously. Praying that this floor plan was the same as the one below, Brent rose to his feet and plunged to his left in search of a door. He barged straight into it, banging his nose painfully. Rubbing the bridge of his nose with his left hand, he groped for a doorknob with his right. He found it and tried turning it clockwise. His heart sank. It was locked.

Unlike the door to Chelga's office, this one did not have panes of glass. In fact, it felt like metal, not wood. More bad news. Brent decided to try forced entry, anyway. He stepped back, raised his right leg, and kicked out viciously at the door. There was a solid, satisfying thud, but the door didn't budge an inch.

Brent tried pounding on the door a few times with his fist. The least he could do would be to warn any tenants. But there was no response from within. Even if there had been a response, it would have been very difficult to hear, for by now, the noise in the burning building was deafening.

Brent stood there a moment, head cocked to one side, and he listened in awe. Dry wood crackled and popped with the volume of gunshots. He had to stifle the impulse to duck when these reports rent the air. The sounds of breaking glass trilled like sopranos in a chorus. And now the crashing sounds of collapsing timbers joined the unholy symphony with greater frequency. And under all of these sounds, like a sustaining bass section, there was the steady, thunderous roar of implacable flames roaming at will in a destructive frenzy.

Then Brent noticed that the color of the smoke was

changing from a uniform gray to a medley of gray and sooty black. The fire must be climbing even more quickly than before. He scurried frantically to the staircase again, leaning his whole right side against the wall this time, to be sure to spot the staircase opening. Where the wall ended and the archway began, he fell sideways and landed painfully on his right hip. This time he didn't bother to get up again, and he simply began to crawl up the steps to the fourth floor.

The roar grew louder, the smoke became even more blinding, and the heat from below surged against his legs and back like a solid presence. His eyelids felt as if they were glued open; he found it hard to blink. His mouth tasted like the inside of a dirty fireplace. And the constant coughing was now producing jet-black sputum. He didn't know where he would get the strength to go on, but he prayed for it to come.

The fourth floor. No more stairs. *Brent's last stand*, he thought grimly. He crawled to his left, head down, searching for the last door, the last chance for survival. His head butted into it and he reached up for the knob. It was locked, of course, but the door felt like wood. On trembling legs, he pulled himself up and summoned his last bit of energy. Taking a painfully deep breath, he backed up a few feet and then surged against the door with his left shoulder.

He crashed through the wooden door panels like a human battering ram, sending chunks and splinters of wood flying into the room before him. The door jerked and shuddered for a second as it made one last valiant effort to bar entry, but it was no match for his desperate momentum. The shattered door swung back on bent hinges and slammed into the wall. He tripped on the edge of the carpet and sprawled headlong onto the floor. He lay there panting and aching for a moment.

The room appeared to be a one-room apartment. Through the thickening smoke loomed a sofa bed and a matching chair. Brent rose to his feet and limped over to the window. The glass on this one was scrupulously clean. He undid the latch and raised the window, which rose easily and smoothly in its track. Good news for a change.

The bad news was apparent as soon as he leaned out the window and saw the dizzying drop. This was a tall, narrow building. Four floors was a long way down. There was no way that a person could jump and not get seriously hurt.

And then he noticed that something was different. The clothes that had been flapping in the wind high overhead when he entered the store were nowhere in sight now. But the clothesline! Would it hold his weight? He reached for the double strand of rope and grasped it in his hand. Not too thick, standard clothesline, but it was nylon. . . .

Before he could adequately analyze his chances, the fire decided for him. A sudden roar behind him made him release the clothesline and spin around. A furious, boiling wall of flame in the hallway outside was forcing its way through the shattered door. In just seconds, this entire room would be an inferno.

He turned back to the window and thrust his right leg up and over the sill. Holding on to the edge of the window frame, he raised his left leg and scooted on his haunches until he was poised precariously on the edge of a four-story drop. Before he could even take a deep breath, he felt himself being pushed into midair by a solid hot blast of air from behind. He didn't even remember reaching for the clothesline, but in another second he found himself hanging from it desperately with both hands, watching it sway and sag above him to a dangerous degree. No time to waste.

He summoned the courage to release the fingers of his left hand. It took an overriding surge of pure willpower. As he let go, suspended now only by the fingers of one hand, he felt himself twisting steadily, uncontrollably, to the right. It was a sickening feeling, and his left hand shot out to grasp the line in front of his right hand. That was the rhythm that needed to be established. Release one hand, hang on with the other, spin momentarily, and then grab for dear life. If only the strength in his fingers held out.

When he was halfway across, his attention was diverted by a crackling and roaring sound behind him. Craning his neck, he could just barely see the window behind him through which he had escaped. Its entire wooden frame was now ablaze and it reminded him of the flaming hoop through which tigers reluctantly jump in the circus. More relevant to his predicament, tongues of flames were licking at the rope from which he hung. It was going to burn through.

Turning back to face the opposite building, Brent renewed his efforts with a fierce determination born of stark fear. He hadn't come this far just to end up squashed on a cobblestone street. But he was only two thirds of the way across when the rope gave way.

One second he was suspended on the swaying rope, and the next second he was plunging downward in an arc toward the opposite wall, still clinging to the rope for all he was worth. As the weatherworn side of the building rushed straight at him, he closed his eyes and gritted his teeth. The impact would probably shatter his legs.

He crashed through the third-floor window and landed on his backside with a massive, bone-jarring thud. If it hadn't been for the thick Oriental carpet, he probably would have fractured his tailbone. As it was, he was dizzy with pain. After a few moments he opened his eyes and looked at his hands. Rigid and bloodless, they were still grasping the rope in a fierce grip. He forced his fingers open and released the rope, letting it slide back over his shoulder.

A furtive movement from the left side of the room caught his eye. Peeking around the corner of a bathroom doorway was a shocked face with eyes as wide as saucers. The man looked Turkish, and he sported a huge, proud mustache that had dabs of shaving cream on it. The man stepped out tentatively from behind the door. He had a large, orange bath towel wrapped around his waist, and in his hand he held an old-fashioned straight razor that he brandished like a weapon. Slack-jawed with astonishment, he stared at this intruder as if he had fallen from the sky.

And so I did, Brent thought. And then he lost consciousness and collapsed in a heap on the stranger's floor.

Brent spent two days in the hospital, being treated for smoke inhalation and a mild concussion. As soon as he was released, he contacted Agency sources via coded satellite transmission to see what they had learned about Etienne and Dr. Carlson.

French officials guardedly admitted having dozens of agents with the name Etienne, but they claimed that none matched the description of the grossly overweight shopkeeper. In fact, they became indignant in their protests that they employed no agent by any name who weighed four hundred pounds. Did Monsieur Collins think that they were running a sideshow? Brent conceded to himself that he might have made an unwarranted assumption in identifying the merchant as Chelga's French spy, whatever his real name. But Brent had no doubt that someone had been pumping an incautious Chelga for information.

As for a Dr. Carlson, even the Agency's deep files, which were privy only to the Director and his first assistant, revealed no agent, friendly or hostile, with that alias in Ethiopia. There was an Irish munitions expert named Carlson in Uganda, but he had never used a medical cover, and two independent sources were positive that he had not traveled out of Uganda since arriving there four months ago.

While the sweep for the unknown doctor continued, Brent was instructed to keep going through his previously assigned list of stringers and full-time agents to check on their loyalty and competence. Chelga's death and the attempt on Brent's life had again driven home the point that the Ethiopian leak needed to be plugged as quickly and as thoroughly as possible.

The situation rankled Brent more than he cared to admit. The idea that someone could betray such a trust and turn double agent was absolutely repugnant to him. It struck him as a vile and reprehensible act. He had more empathy and understanding for flat-out, committed enemy agents than he could ever have for a turncoat. Like himself, those agents were putting themselves on the line for their personal beliefs, however alien those beliefs might be to him. A turncoat, on the other hand, seemed to have no center, no core. A turncoat was a hollow opportunist. A turncoat would sell out a colleague for a buck or for a hit of some narcotic.

Brent was perfectly aware that there was a personal element involved here. It was a turncoat who had almost gotten him killed that night on the road to Medellin. It was a friend and colleague, enslaved by a heroin habit, who had told the cartel where Brent would be, who had described the car even down to its phony license-plate number. No matter that the turncoat had been discovered and summarily dispatched. There was a sacred principle involved here, a vital moral and social code, and its shabby violation had shaken Brent to his core.

Unless he actively fought the impulse, he now found it easy to slip into cynicism or despair. He had acquired a sense of wariness and disconnection. It was as if he moved among others encased in a bubble of doubt. He began to suspect that everything was appearance, that there was no such thing as reality. The feeling was alienating, it was isolating, and ultimately it was deeply demoralizing. What was the purpose of all this activity if everyone insisted on playing by his or her own twisted rules? What made life anything more than a cruel cosmic joke?

He shook his head to clear away these unproductive thoughts. For the moment, there was nothing to do except go through the old, familiar motions and wait for illumination. If the dark veil failed to lift—well, he would deal with that in an appropriate way when the time came.

Brent sat now in a third-floor room in a hotel that catered to foreign businessmen. He turned his attention to the materials scattered on the desk in front of him. He needed to rearrange the contents of a bulky sample case to get ready for his next interview.

He had decided that this phase of the probe would focus on a stringer named Halima Legassa. A department head in the Bureau of Public Works in the capital city, she was an invaluable asset because of the nature of her job and because of her superior abilities. Unlike Chelga's personnel file back in Washington, which had been embarrassingly slim, hers was crammed with laudatory assessments. But if she was of great value to American interests, certainly she could be of great value to her own country's interests too.

Brent shuffled through the computer disks, matching each set with its spiral-bound documentation. He was using his normal cover, that of a systems adviser for a computer firm specializing in municipal software. The company was real and so was the software, which enjoyed brisk sales and had an international reputation. But most of the software had been developed by Agency computer specialists, of whom Brent was one. The Agency-owned company could offer cities and municipalities computer programs that would inventory city equipment, run payroll departments, supervise infrastructure repair schedules, and provide a host of other services.

Unlike other duties, such as surveillance, Brent found this aspect of his work congenial and challenging. He enjoyed tackling complex problems and using his computer expertise to solve them. Of course, it didn't hurt that many of the programs he installed could also snare information from other disks booted into a computer. Some programs even contained deadly computer viruses that, when deliberately activated, could shut down vital city operations. These days, sabotage could be compressed into a microchip.

Brent was certain that Halima Legassa did not know that he was coming to see her in a dual capacity. She simply knew that in the course of a recent telephone call, a company representative had touted an interesting new program that would allow her department to coordinate and map the city's complex underground maze of electrical and communications lines. This afternoon, he would make a general presentation to Ms. Legassa and her staff. He would have to watch for an opening to get her alone.

Having gathered the materials he would need, Brent took a shower and changed into a tropical-weight business suit. A look out the window told him that he had better carry a raincoat just in case. Dark clouds were scudding across the sky.

If Brent's ability to read a crowd was holding up, the presentation had been a success. Ms. Legassa had translated for those who spoke no English, so no one had been left out. The features offered by his computer programs had neatly anticipated the needs expressed by the audience, and many intelligent questions had been asked along the way. As usual, a couple of the people in the back row closed their heavy lids and nodded off to sleep, but Brent had been at this long enough to know that if no more than ten percent fell asleep, his performance could be counted as a success.

After the presentation Brent met with Halima Legassa and her two chief assistants. One of them was a plump, older man in an ill-fitting suit who kept mopping his brow with a handkerchief even though the computer room was air-conditioned. The other assistant was a young woman in a tailored, Western-style business suit. Ms. Legassa herself was more traditionally attired in the long togalike garment called a *shama*. Now that the general presentation was over, it was hard-sell time, and these were the people who really needed to be convinced. Brent was seated at a computer terminal, demonstrating some of the more sophisticated features of the software.

"Okay," he said. "Now, this menu allows you to assign a different color *and* a different thickness to each of the lines representing a utility pipe. You can see how that produces an easier-to-read graphic representation of your underground system." He stroked a key combination, and his small audience leaned closer to admire the result.

Fifteen minutes later the young female assistant respectfully motioned her department head aside and spoke to her quietly. At the end of the brief conversation, Ms. Legassa nodded and returned to the computer desk as the other woman left the room.

"Ms. Ashagire has asked me to express her appreciation for your presentation, Mr. Collins. She regrets that she must leave, but today is payday for our employees and she must attend to her distribution duties." She smiled graciously. "We do use your company's payroll program, of course. It is very accurate."

"I'm pleased to hear that. I think you'll find that *all* our programs are accurate and reliable." Brent wasn't about to say so, but that particular payroll program also allowed the Agency to get an accurate picture of the number and placement of many government employees in Third World countries.

He turned back casually to the keyboard, then paused as if a new thought had just occurred to him, though in fact he had been holding it in reserve. "Ms. Legassa, if you would allow me to enter a small sector of your actual installations in these graphics, I think it would help you to see what this program can do for your department."

Ms. Legassa tilted her head to one side as she considered the matter. Then she turned to her other assistant and said, "Mr. Teferi, would you be kind enough to bring us a utilities blueprint from the chart room? Any sector will do." With a slight bow, the plump assistant rushed off in search of the document. This was Brent's chance. He fiddled with a hidden section of the program, and within seconds, the computer speaker was emitting white noise that would effectively block any hidden microphones. The sudden intrusion seemed to annoy Ms. Legassa.

"Hickory, dickory, dock." He delivered the words seriously and urgently, looking her straight in the eye.

Ms. Legassa was obviously startled. She took a slight step backward, and her hand flew involuntarily to her throat. She stared at Brent for a moment until she recovered her composure. Then she looked quickly around the empty room and responded in a hoarse whisper: "Ding, dong, dell."

Brent nodded in satisfaction. Most people, if they knew the children's rhyme, would have responded, "The

mouse ran up the clock.'' But Ms. Legassa knew the
proper code.

"Mr. Collins, I had no idea. . . .'' She seemed to be
stunned by Brent's unexpected revelation.

"There was no reason why you should have. In fact,
if you *had* known, I would have been worried about losing
my touch.'' He glanced quickly at the door to the hallway.
"Please come closer. Listen, we don't have much time.
Can you tell me anything about a French agent named
Etienne? A man who weighs about four hundred
pounds?'' He caught himself using the wrong measure-
ment system. "Sorry, make that about a hundred and
eighty kilograms.''

A stricken look crossed her face. "Surely you mean
the man we call Yämärgän—the malediction.'' She spat
the name out. "But he is not French. He is Cuban. Yes,
I know of him. He has practically taken over our secret
police. Thanks to him, we know a reign of terror. He is
a scourge upon my people, Mr. Collins—a curse! I hope
for your sake that you will have no dealings with him.''

"I'm afraid that I may have had a run-in with him
already, but I survived, as you can see.'' Brent shifted
in his chair. "Tell me—has this Yämärgän or anyone
else expressed any undue interest in you recently? What
I mean is, have you felt that you were being followed or
that your phone was being tapped? Has anyone hinted
that your loyalty might not be what it could be? Anything
at all that struck you as being hostile or out of the ordinary?''

She smiled wryly. "All of the above, Mr. Collins.
After all, this is a police state, you know. We *are* followed, and our phones *are* tapped. We are always being

urged toward more orthodoxy. This is not paranoia; this is a fact of life.''

"I appreciate that, but I mean a recent intensification, anything that might lead you to believe that you've become an object of attention in a way that wasn't true before.''

She shrugged. "I do not think so. But it would be difficult to tell. You see, those of us who work for the government always receive more attention than the ordinary citizen.''

She turned her head apprehensively and Brent looked up in frustration as they both heard heavy footsteps scurrying back down the hall. "The name Dr. Carlson—does that mean anything to you?''

A light of recognition flashed in her eyes, but before she could answer, her assistant was entering the room, a long set of blueprints cradled carefully in his arms like a baby. Brent cursed under his breath and turned off the covering background noise. If Teferi weren't such an eager beaver, Brent might now know who the elusive Dr. Carlson was. He would have to wait for another opportunity.

But as he turned back to his demonstration, it occurred to Brent that too many sessions alone with Ms. Legassa could put her in grave danger. This Yämärgän would know him on sight, and he was probably monitoring all of his movements and noting the contacts that he made. This was standard procedure when an American entered the country. Brent knew that his story was plausible enough. After all, it would not be unusual for a foreign businessman to hire the services of a local translator. And his presence here today was perfectly covered by the services he was rendering. But he knew the eroding power of too much coincidence. In its presence, even the most convincing cover would begin to crumble.

So Brent dropped any further thought of isolating Ms. Legassa. Instead, he deliberately violated business protocol and began to direct his pitch to the assistant, Teferi. If Ms. Legassa was as sharp as her dossier indicated, Brent was certain that she would catch on to what he was doing and play along. If he could now make it seem that his primary focus was her assistant, it would work to her advantage. And, indeed, as he cultivated Teferi, who was naturally flattered by the attention, he caught sight of Ms. Legassa using the opportunity to write something surreptitiously on the back of a sales-order slip.

Finally, Teferi ran out of questions and Brent sensed that the session had come to a natural end. He pumped Teferi's hand warmly, thanked him profusely for his attention, and gathered up his materials. He left the usual sample disk and short documentation with Ms. Legassa, whom he also thanked, but less vociferously, and then he headed back to his rented car.

When he was back in his hotel room and safely behind locked doors, he searched through his sales forms until he found the one with the spidery handwriting on the back. It read: *Dr. Carlson—American scientist—ethology. Should now be in Lake Abaya region.*

Brent smiled. This was the break that he had been waiting for, and using a priority code, he placed an urgent order with headquarters for a Land Rover equipped for extensive camping and surveillance. It was time to do some stalking in the wild.

Chapter Three

There is nothing worse than the smell of a jackal's breath. Brent came to that conclusion as he lay sprawled helplessly on his back, the jaws of a jackal clamped around his throat. As he lay there motionless, he could feel a steady trickle of animal saliva running down the right side of his throat, sliding under the collar of his shirt, and pooling behind his neck. No doubt the collar would be stained. And it would be incredibly foul-smelling. What on earth had this jackal eaten for its last meal? Brent's stomach lurched as he considered the possibilities. Better not to know. But whatever it was, Fido here had definitely forgotten to brush.

Half an hour earlier, Brent had stopped to reconnoiter in what looked like a very safe place. It was the relatively flat top of a huge boulder, and it had taken him a few minutes to work his way up there by carefully choosing handholds and toeholds in the fissures and cracks. There was even the rare luxury of a clump of scrub brush on top. Aside from giving him some small shelter against the onslaught of the midday sun, it also offered a degree of cover. He could peer around the brush and see the mountains of the Ethiopian Highlands looming behind him. In front of him, he had an unobstructed view of the valley leading to Lake Abaya. Best of all, he could not easily be seen by prying eyes as he searched for traces of Dr. Carlson's camp.

He had eaten some dates from his backpack and taken two precious swallows of water from his near-empty canteen. Then he had stretched out on his stomach and applied his glare-free field glasses to the valley below.

The next thing that he knew, his bush hat was being nudged from his head by a long snout. When he rolled over defensively, he found himself staring up into an unrelenting pair of glistening brown eyes. Before he could move again, the jackal had straddled his chest and fastened its teeth around his throat.

The animal was no larger than a medium-sized dog. It was certainly possible to pick it up and hurl it from this rock to a certain death below, but Brent was unwilling to pay the price. The jackal's eyes were evidently watching Brent's outstretched arms with careful attention. Brent deduced that from the fact that the jaws clamped a little tighter every time that he began to move his hand or flex his fingers.

Now Brent could hear the unmistakable click and scrabble of claws as other jackals began to work their way up the bare sides of the boulder where he was trapped. He remembered, with a sinking feeling, that they always traveled in packs. The jackal who had him pinned down growled menacingly at the others, and Brent could feel the eerily ticklish vibrations running up and down his throat. Another blast of foul breath assailed his nostrils as the jackal growled again, this time with even more ferocity. Then it turned its head slightly in the direction of its nearest challenger, and Brent could feel the sharp fangs scrape the skin of his neck. He turned his head carefully to keep in sync with the jackal's movement. The longer he could avoid that moment when its fangs began to rend and tear his flesh, the better.

But then, without warning, the jackal pushed off from Brent's chest and launched itself through the air in an athletic leap at its competitor. Brent was stunned by the speed of the whole operation. One second he had been pinned down, and now he was free. He leaped to his feet and looked around desperately on the ground for something he could use as a weapon. From the corner of his eye, he could see two jackals tumbling end over end in combat, a rolling tangle of snarls and fury.

He rejected the field glasses as a weapon. But that rock over there—the one shaped like a cantaloupe—just the thing! He scrambled desperately for it and closed his hands around it. He hefted the sun-warmed rock in his palms, satisfied by its weight and its size. Then he raised it high over his head and spun around to face his attacker. Startled by what he saw, he nearly dropped the rock on his own skull.

Perched on a ledge twenty yards away was a woman in her late twenties. She was dressed in tan shirt and shorts. Her blond hair was pulled back behind her head and secured in a short ponytail. She was watching the whole scene intently and scribbling furiously into a notebook.

That really got to him: Here he was, being mauled by wild animals, while the woman was casually taking notes as if it were a classroom lecture. He hurled the rock angrily to the ground at his feet. The jackals froze in their tracks; the woman dropped her pen.

"You've startled the pack!" Her tone was accusatory.

He looked at her incredulously. "I've startled the pack? They creep up on me and try to rip my throat out, and you say that *I* have startled *them?* Get real, lady!"

"They weren't going to hurt you. They were just—"

"Not going to hurt me?" He rubbed his throat. "I've got marks here that say otherwise. Look, I don't know how long you've been sitting there, but you must have missed the performance of that fleabag over there." He pointed to the larger jackal, standing defiantly at the head of the pack. "Dog Breath there tried to *kill* me!"

She shook her head in exasperation. "Don't call him that. His name is Starback." She paused, then brought the thumb and first finger of her right hand to her lips and gave a piercing whistle. Instantly, the lead jackal broke into a lope and headed straight for her.

Oh, no! Brent thought in alarm. *Now it's going to attack her!* Reacting instinctively, he bent down for the rock he had hurled to the ground in disgust. But before he could even wrap his fingers around it, the jackal had already bounded across the intervening distance and reached her feet. It stood looking up at her expectantly.

She smiled sweetly at Brent. "Oh, you're right. There's no doubt about this one. He's a genuine killer, all right."

From his bent-over position, Brent sank the rest of the way to the hard ground and plopped down. This was going to be a very long day.

* * *

As it turned out, Dr. Carlson's first name was Melissa. As Halima Legassa had hastily written, she was American and she was an ethologist. Brent had looked up the term before starting this trip. It referred to a scientist who studied animal behavior. *Her* specialty was jackals.

They sat now in the twilight by a campfire near her tent. Brent had found it an easy matter to convince her that he was doing some free-lance writing and photography for *Personality,* a shallow but extremely popular newsmagazine that sold well in airports and supermarkets. He was interested, he told her, in using her and her work as a subject.

At first, she had been totally unimpressed about the prospect of being profiled in a national magazine. Her ego didn't seem to be inflated enough for Brent to use to his advantage. But when he reminded her that the magazine had played a pivotal role in boosting many a scientist's ability to raise funds for research, she perked up considerably. Brent smiled to himself. He had never yet heard of a researcher who didn't need more money.

Now Brent was probing gently for information. He still didn't know how she fit into the picture. "So then you met Halima Legassa at a private college in Addis Ababa," he prompted.

"That's right. That's where I teach a course in field techniques once a year to exchange students as part of my funding requirements. It's an extension program of Stanford's—my alma mater and my chief sponsor. Halima is on the board of directors of the private college. She's a very accomplished woman. I really admire her."

Brent decided to stretch the truth, and he said, "Well, she expressed admiration for you, too, when I interviewed her earlier this week. In fact, she's the one who put me on to you as a potential subject for an article.'' Brent watched incredulously as Melissa actually blushed. He couldn't remember the last time that he had seen that kind of modesty. It was very becoming. But then, to an accomplished actress, it could also be a very disarming weapon.

''So, do you spend a lot of time in Addis Ababa teaching? I mean, that would cut way down on your time for field studies, wouldn't it?''

''It certainly would. And that would drive me absolutely crazy.'' She indicated the plains and hills around them with a sweep of her hand. ''This is where I love to be, doing primary research. No, the lectures at the college take up just the first two weeks of the semester. Then I pack up all the students and transport them right to this site for some hands-on learning. That's the best part of the course, as far as I'm concerned. I just don't know of any better teacher than harsh reality.''

''I can certainly buy that. So I gather, then, that you spend most of your time right here and not very much in the city.''

''That's right. I do range around a bit, depending on the movements of the pack of jackals, but during the last year it's stayed roughly within a two-mile radius of this camp. Once a pack stakes out its territory, it usually takes a natural disaster like a drought to make it move.''

So far, Brent could detect neither wariness nor evasiveness in Dr. Carlson's answers. She seemed to be what she said she was. But he intended to corroborate that later. Now he shifted his attention to any connection that she might have with Ethiopian nationals or authorities.

"It must be difficult to keep up with a pack on the move, even if they do stick to a two-mile radius. Do you have to hire local people to help you, or is this pretty much a one-person operation?"

Her eyes swept the small compound. "What you see is what you get. I don't have the funding to hire a permanent staff. I do get some temporary help from the students, of course, but that's seasonal." She smiled ruefully. "And not always as helpful as I would like."

"Well, being self-sufficient has its advantages, of course." Brent leaned forward to explain: "I mean, it strikes me that it might be hard to get local help even if you could afford it. Ever since I arrived, I've had the impression that being from the U.S. is sort of a drawback around here. We don't seem to be on their favored-nation list. How do you handle the anti-American feeling that you run into? Or doesn't it affect you out here in the boonies?"

"I've run into some of it in the city, of course. You must have seen the posters and read the newspapers when you were there. But the strange thing is that it seldom seems to be personal. I mean, there's a lot of rhetoric against America and all, but I've never had it directed against me in particular. And out here in the countryside, people seem to be a lot less political. They're more worried about simple survival."

"So you've never been hassled by officials or bothered by your neighbors?"

She shook her head. "Maybe it's the nature of my work. There's no way that it can be misinterpreted as political or antigovernment. In fact, I've got official government backing and protection for my ethology studies.

It makes them look good in the eyes of the international community—concern for natural resources, and all that. They're even footing part of the bill. A very small part, unfortunately. And the local tribesmen seem to be more amused than annoyed by me.''

''Amused? Why would they be amused?''

''They think that it's hilarious that anyone would want to study jackals, of all things. But it's all good-natured. I even get the feeling that they keep a protective eye on me.''

''Why *do* you study jackals, of all things?''

''Because they're fascinating, absolutely fascinating. I love observing them and recording their behavior. And I'm just ecstatic over being accepted by them to the point where they let me get so close. I really had to work at that. But if you mean why did I choose them as my field of study, it was the usual graduate-school dilemma: All the sexy animals were already taken. Goodall had the chimps, Fossey had the gorillas, Adamson had the lions. Everybody on earth was saving the elephants. So I decided that Melissa Carlson was going to have the jackals all to herself.''

Their attention was drawn to the campfire as a branch collapsed and sent a noisy shower of sparks scurrying briefly into the twilight air. Brent looked over at Melissa inquiringly. ''Shall I add another branch to the fire?''

She pulled the collar of her jacket up behind her neck. ''Yes, I think that's a good idea. I can feel the temperature starting its usual nighttime plunge.''

Brent walked over to a mounded stack of wood, mostly twigs and small branches, and then he rooted through it for a larger piece. His fingers were just closing around a branch when the faintest of sounds caught his attention. He looked up and over the woodpile and into a pair of glowing eyes. The effect was hypnotic on both man and beast.

Staring wordlessly into the jackal's eyes was one of the strangest sensations that he had ever experienced. There was something absolutely alien about this creature; Brent felt in his bones that it was totally *other*. But at the same time, there was some kind of primitive kinship between them. On this night and in this place, they were fellow passengers on spaceship earth. And strangest sensation of all, he felt almost certain that these same thoughts were running through the mind of this animal.

It seemed to Brent that they stayed frozen in place for hours, looking through the windows of each other's soul, but, in fact, the contact lasted for perhaps a minute. Then the jackal broke eye contact and began to move in a wide arc around him as it circled toward where Melissa sat.

Brent turned slowly as he watched the jackal's quiet and stately approach. He felt no need to warn Melissa. He simply knew that there was no danger either to himself or to her. He watched as Melissa caught sight of the jackal and broke into a smile.

"Good evening, Starback. And how are you tonight? Was the hunting good today?" The jackal watched her face with unswerving attention, turning its head slightly to one side and cocking its ears. Brent had no romanticized illusions about the scene before him. He knew that the jackal was assessing the tone of Melissa's voice, not understanding her words. But the bond between them was amazing.

And then the jackal did a curious and, to Brent, a

disgusting thing. It walked to within six inches of Melissa's feet, lowered its head, and regurgitated something on the ground. Melissa seemed neither surprised nor disgusted. In fact, as Brent watched, she reached down with her bare hand and picked up what looked like the body of a mouse.

And then, to Brent's amazement, she emitted a series of high-pitched squeaks. Apparently satisfied, the jackal wagged its tail, turned, and instantly disappeared into the night. After a half minute, Melissa rose from her chair, walked over to the underbrush that fringed her camp, and dropped the body of the mouse into it.

She wiped her hand on her jeans and turned toward Brent. ''Well, that takes care of my bedtime snack.''

''That was amazing. I've never seen anything like it.''

''No, I suppose you haven't. In fact, few people ever have. Thanks for not scaring him off, Brent. I should have warned you that this is a nightly ritual.''

''It's okay. I was able to piece it together.''

He placed another branch in the fire and they returned to their camp chairs.

''I suppose you gathered that Starback was feeding me the way that jackals feed their pups. He doesn't think too much of my hunting abilities. I've never been quick enough to catch a mouse—thank heaven!''

''So he looks upon you as sort of the daughter he never had?''

Melissa laughed. ''I suppose you could put it that way, although he already has dozens of sons and daughters. He's the dominant male in the pack.''

''Tell me about the pack.'' Brent leaned forward, his interest piqued in a way that would not have been possible before witnessing the strange encounter between beauty and the beast.

And so they talked enthusiastically well into the night. Finally they retired, she to her tent and he to the sleeping bag in the back of his Land Rover. It occurred to him, as he drifted off to sleep, that even though he still didn't know how Melissa's name had been dragged into all of this, he was inclined to trust her. Somehow, that was a relief.

Brent found himself humming the theme song from "Sesame Street" as he maneuvered his way along what passed as a highway some miles northeast of Melissa's camp. He puzzled over the significance of the song for a few minutes, and then he dropped the matter with a shrug.

He had spent an interesting day with Melissa, learning more about jackals than he ever thought he would want to know. And he had learned just enough about Melissa to want to know more. She fascinated him. She was intelligent, self-sufficient in a very hostile environment, and filled with a wealth of firsthand knowledge. Next to her, the women he had been dating back in the States seemed so shallow, so frivolous.

He was inclined to believe that she had nothing to do with Chelga or—more to the point—with Yämärgän. But he was still puzzled as to how her name had gotten mixed up in this. Perhaps just being American was enough to qualify a person as a potential spy and to invite suspicion. Perhaps Yämärgän was perfectly aware that she was innocuous, but found her foreign name convenient to use when picking Chelga's brain. It was hard to say.

He slammed on the brakes to avoid hitting a large animal that darted suddenly across the rubble-strewn trail. The deerlike creature bounded effortlessly through the air and disappeared into the brush on the other side of the road. As he sat there, hands gripping the steering wheel, two more of them crossed the road, half running and, it seemed, half flying. A memory clicked into place. Melissa had spoken of a rare antelope that lived in this region. The size, the coloration—these had to be nyala antelope. *But if they keep leaping into traffic like that,* Brent thought, *they'll become even rarer.*

He shifted gears and continued to bounce along the road. Within the hour he should reach his next destination, the site for a dam project on a tributary of the Juba River. In fact, he was running considerably early for his appointment. Back once again in his capacity as computer systems adviser, he was scheduled to meet with the dam's chief consulting engineer, a man named Ken Horton. Horton's Philadelphia firm had been hired by the Ethiopian government to deal with some tricky problems in hydrodynamics. Brent remembered a remark that Melissa had made. Here was another case where the official anti-American rhetoric didn't seem to stop the government from turning to American know-how when they needed it. Anyway, Brent had to check out some software adaptation glitches for Horton. He also had to check out Horton himself. Horton was a fellow agent.

Having time to spare, Brent began looking for an oasis or a picturesque area where he could stop for lunch. A few miles farther on, he spotted a glint of water from a marsh pond over to his right about a quarter of a mile off the road. It would require leaving the road and he would have to be cautious, but he had gained confidence and respect for the abilities of the Land Rover.

He eased slowly off the hard surface of the highway and onto the softer turf of the moorland plateau. He looked out his open window in curiosity at the soil over which his tires were creeping. He remembered Melissa's explaining how all this topsoil was due to the work of one creature—the mole rat. These furry rodents, which could weigh up to two pounds, spent most of their life under the surface, plowing the soil they created and sustained by their own waste materials. He found this an apt parallel to the kind of human mole that he was seeking.

Suddenly he began to feel a subtle difference in his handling of the Rover. It was barely perceptible, but he had the distinct feeling that a slight sliding or fishtailing was going on. He decided not to take any chances, and he came to a halt and leaned out the window to get a better look at the left front tire. Sure enough, there was some mud caked on the sidewalls. The terrain was getting marshy. This was close enough. He turned the key and killed the motor. Now he could focus on his surroundings instead of on his driving.

Dead ahead was the oasis. A large, kidney-shaped pond formed its focal point, but it was surrounded by tall vegetation and trees. Most noticeable at first were the towering lobelias that soared almost fifteen feet high and were capped by colorful flower spikes. But then the birds caught his eye with their darting movements and flashes of color. He recognized sunbirds, siskins, and thrushes as they engaged in feeding and play and conflict. In the shallow pond, cranes lifted their impossibly slender legs to move to more advantageous feeding positions. And as he watched, a flock of blue-winged geese circled, warning everyone with loud honks that they were about to land, ready or not.

Suddenly, five jackals emerged cautiously from cover and moved down to the water's edge. Struck by the beauty of the scene, Brent reached back over the seat for his camera. Then he opened the door noiselessly and stepped down. The ground was squishy beneath his boots. It was a good thing that he had driven no farther. After looking through the camera viewfinder, Brent decided to creep just a little closer to the oasis. It was obvious that the jackals and the birds had sensed his presence already, but they seemed to be nervously tolerant of him for the moment.

Ever so slowly, he eased himself closer. But as he crept along, he had to make a greater effort with each step to lift his feet. Suction was pulling against his boots. Puzzled, he stood in place for a moment. As he watched, the sole ridge of his boots disappeared from sight. Soon, mud oozed over the toecaps, and then *they* disappeared. With alarming rapidity, he found himself sinking deeper into the mire. Expending significant effort, he pulled his left leg out.

The loud gurgling and plopping sound alarmed the jackals, and they streaked back into the brush. Their movement set up a general panic, and hundreds of birds rose into the air as one, shrieking alarms. The air was suddenly filled with desperation, a feeling that Brent now shared, and he knew that he had to work himself back to the Land Rover without delay.

Straining all the way, he managed to take three more steps to turn around. He didn't like what he saw. The vehicle had acquired a slight but definite tilt to the left. It, too, was sinking. Brent cursed under his breath. He had been stupid. Leaving an established trail was a foolhardy thing to do in these parts. Well, nothing for it now but to get out of here and back on the road.

But try as he might, he couldn't summon enough strength to escape the clutches of the forces that held him and pulled him down. He was sinking in material that felt like quivering dirt. It was some kind of amalgam of soil and vegetation and water. With a start, Brent finally realized what it was. It was quicksand.

Chapter Four

B rent renewed his efforts in earnest, pulling against powerful forces that seemed to have acquired a personal malevolence. He had now sunk in up to his knees. In vain, he grabbed his right thigh in both hands and tried to pull as his leg muscles strained upward with all the power he could summon. He felt the boot begin to slide from his foot. No matter, he would gladly give up a boot in order to escape from this morass.

But the more he struggled, the faster he began to sink. It felt like an old freight elevator that takes a shuddering moment or two to gain momentum and then moves steadily downward. Exhaustion momentarily brought Brent's frantic struggle to a halt. He could now feel wetness at his beltline. Then, as he stood there helplessly, a long-forgotten memory of a survival technique sprang unbidden into his mind. Chest-deep now, he acted on that memory and extended his arms straight out at his sides and turned them palm downward. Something told him that this would slow down his sinking motion.

From somewhere out of the past, he had a sharp mental

image of a man trapped in quicksand who had executed this same maneuver. As if it were a movie, Brent could picture the man extending his arms, sinking up to his shoulders, and then stopping. It was worth the effort. Anything was worth the effort.

As he felt the chilling wetness touch the undersides of his arms, he remembered where he had seen this technique. It had shown up on late-night television in a Tarzan movie—a stupid Tarzan movie! The ludicrousness of it all suddenly hit him, and involuntarily he burst into a hearty laugh. He stood there, arms extended and slowly disappearing, and caused the quicksand to undulate with his laughter. If this was it, if it was all over, he might as well go out laughing.

"I must say, you are receiving this in good humor, old chap."

The laughter died in Brent's throat as the British accent skimmed over the marshland to his ears. His eyes snapped open to see a light-skinned black man, dressed in a flowing white garment, standing with one foot on the running board of the tilted Land Rover. As Brent watched, the man leaped nimbly into the driver's seat and brought the engine to life.

Brent watched in astonishment and horror as the man began to back the Land Rover out of the quagmire. He was actually going to take Brent's car and leave him here to die! Brent was outraged. He opened his mouth to yell, but clamped his mouth shut again as he felt wetness on the bottom of his chin. So much for Tarzan and his life-saving technique. In spite of his extended arms, he was already up to his neck in quicksand.

He watched helplessly as the thief played the gears and

modulated the accelerator in an attempt to take the Land Rover. Little by little, slipping and sliding, the vehicle strained backward in its attempt to reach solid ground. Finally, evidently satisfied, the man stopped the Land Rover and jumped back out. Moving quickly but with an economy of motion, he approached the front bumper and began to fiddle with something. Brent felt a surge of outrage. Here he was about to die, and this heartless thief was concerned only about the car.

"So, now. When I direct you this rope, acquire it with one hand. Only the one hand, do you know? This is important."

Eagerly, Brent began to nod, but the disgusting taste of slime on his lips brought his head motion to an instantaneous halt. He watched the man uncoil the rest of the rope, one end of which was now tied to the front bumper, and begin to twirl it in the air.

With an intensity of focus that he had never before experienced and would not have believed possible, Brent watched the rope snake through the air. It seemed to him that he could clearly see the three separate intertwined strands that formed the rope. He could even see the fuzzy fibers that stuck out like wisps of unruly hair. And when the rope slapped against the wet surface, each drop of fleeing water was distinctly visible to him. He could have counted them.

The rope lay four feet or so in front of him. Able to breathe only through his nostrils now, he began to summon the enormous effort that would be needed to pull his right hand free. But before he could move, the rope began to slide away from him.

"One minute, please. The distance from you is too much. I will attempt again."

Brent willed the man to hurry, to retrieve the rope with the speed of lightning, and to send it on its life-giving way in a fraction of a second. But it seemed to take an eternity. The rope ambled back toward the Land Rover in slow motion, like a leisurely old snake with a very full stomach. Brent's nostrils were now filled with the fetid odor of marsh water. When his nose went under, it would all be over.

Again his rescuer began to twirl the rope in the air like an Ethiopian version of a cowboy. Again he released it at the edge of its arc. And again it flew through the air with amazing clarity. This time it plopped right in front of Brent's face, splattering his eyelids and forehead with muddy residue. Reaching to the core of his being, Brent summoned the strength to pull his right arm from the muck and he watched as it surged smoothly into the air, flinging drops in all directions. It seemed to him that his arm was disembodied, that it had a life of its own. He watched admiringly as it headed unerringly for the rope and curled its fingers around it. At the first sensation of contact, the hand belonged to him again. He closed his fingers tightly around the rope.

"So, now. When you attach with the other hand, your face will . . . what is the word? Ah! Your face will submersing. You know? So, the very big breath."

In spite of the man's idiosyncratic version of English, Brent understood him perfectly. Removing his other arm and leaning toward the rope would shift his center of gravity, and he would tilt toward a more horizontal position. He could expect his face to go under.

Brent watched as the man returned to the Land Rover and vaulted up into the driver's seat. Then he leaned out the open window, held his left arm out for a few seconds to get Brent's attention, and then dropped it, making a furious circular motion with his hand.

Brent pulled his left arm noisily upward out of the mire and grasped the rope just below his right hand. As the Land Rover began to move in reverse and the rope began to grow taut, Brent took a deep breath like a swimmer about to catapult from a diving board. As he surged forward, he felt his face dip into the wetness.

The quicksand did not give up easily. Engulfed in wet darkness, he felt his other boot being ripped off his foot. For a moment, it seemed that the force of the suction engaged in this brutal tug-of-war would pull his very skin off. But mechanical power won, and Brent bobbed to the surface like a cork, his lungs gulping in the precious gift of air. Now he was skimming over the surface like a human surfboard, head straining high. Having reached the road, the Land Rover came to a screeching halt, and Brent's forward momentum stopped abruptly.

He lay on his stomach for a moment, arms almost wrenched out of their sockets, lungs heaving with exertion, and skin stinging with multiple scrapes and friction burns. But he was alive. Thank God, he was alive.

His rescuer was named Yakob Fankara, and he was a goatherd. Brent spent the next hour cleaning up at Yakob's nearby hut, a mud and thatchwork structure attached to a small cave that served as a sheltered corral for his goats. Yakob had been grazing them on the moorland when he came upon Brent and his predicament.

Several times, Brent expressed his gratitude to Yakob for having saved his life. But Yakob modestly shrugged off Brent's gratitude, saying simply that fate had put him in the right place at the right time. As he picturesquely put it, "When the odor is in the wind, any nose will do." Yakob came across as a simple, cheerful goatherd.

But later, as Brent bumped and bucked over the rutted road on his way to his appointment with Ken Horton, he couldn't help speculating on the ancient riddle of appearance versus reality. For instance, the moorland appeared to be solid enough to walk on. In reality, it was treacherous and deadly. So why would an experienced goatherd take his flock there to graze?

And though Yakob appeared to be just a simple peasant, he spoke English, something that an uneducated peasant would not be expected to know. And when Brent had idly looked into the corral during milking time, he had noticed Yakob hastily throwing a burlap sack over what looked suspiciously like a radio transmitter at the back of the goat cave.

Brent didn't know what to make of his rescuer. All that he knew was that Yakob Fankara's name was not on his list of agents and stringers. Whose list he was on remained a mystery.

Like the bones of some huge prehistoric animal, the framing timbers and forms of the half-finished concrete dam jutted up out of the floor of the river valley at a rakish angle. Ken Horton gestured offhandedly in the direction of the structure and he told Brent, "It's the crazy shift in climate that does the mischief. For nine, ten months of the year, things are bone dry around here.

You look at a dam like this and you wonder why it's sitting there in the first place. Then comes the rainy season, like now, and huge walls of water come racing down the riverbed with no warning and they sweep everything out of their path.'' He shook his head in disgust. ''It's going to be one humongous challenge to make the footing strong enough to withstand the compression. What they should have done was call me in earlier to design that base.''

Brent glanced sideways at Horton as he complained about the project. In his late forties, Horton was deeply tanned and his face was heavily lined, testimony to a life spent outdoors in the harsh sun. When he reached up and took off his yellow hard hat to scratch his head, he uncovered a shiny scalp surrounded by a fringe of coarse brown hair. His heavily mirrored sunglasses hid both the color of his eyes and any expression they might reveal.

''I can see that the base of the dam is about three times as wide as the top,'' Brent said. ''You'd think that would be enough to hold.'' He looked curiously at the partly finished dam. ''But aside from this location, why bother to stop the water at all? It must have been rushing through this valley for thousands of years, at least. What is there to save downstream?''

Horton shook his head impatiently. ''It's got nothing to do with saving anything downstream. This is basically an agricultural project.'' He pointed to the valley upstream of the dam. ''What they're proposing to do is to flood that entire portion of the valley and turn it into a giant reservoir. Then, when the dry season hits, the water can be parceled out to farmers.''

Brent scanned the horizon. "That's odd. I didn't see any farms around here when I was driving in."

"There aren't any . . . yet. But the government is planning a huge relocation project. They intend to break up the densely populated areas where food is scarce and turn people into producers instead of just consumers. They want to make this area the breadbasket of their country. They should have got it going years ago."

Brent was taken aback. "But that sounds like what happened in China a few years back, when they forcibly moved people out of the cities and into the remote provinces."

"Sure, or what happened in Kampuchea when it stopped being called Cambodia. But, then, they're not into freedom of choice around here, Collins. Or haven't you noticed?"

There it was again, that sneering tone that had come up a few times earlier in the course of their conversation, and which seemed to be a permanent feature of Horton's personality. It was beginning to grate on Brent's nerves, but he let it pass. He looked around unobtrusively to make sure that no one was within earshot and then he said, "Let me fly something by you. Those recent troop movements around here that you mentioned earlier—do you think that they're connected in any way to this relocation plan?"

"Sure, that's part of what they're all about. There are a lot of nomads in these parts, and nomads have a nasty habit of crossing political boundaries freely. That makes them a threat to a government that's trying to control its people. So I think that these troop movements are signs that they're about to establish stricter border control. I expect to see barbed-wire installations, patrol towers, all the usual garbage. At least, that's what they should do if they're serious." He pulled off his hard hat and scratched his head again. "And another thing those troops are about is putting down revolution with a vengeance."

"Around here? But I thought that the rebels were clustered up in the northern provinces."

"Yeah, that's where most of the fighting has taken place up to now. But I get the impression that rebel supply bases have widened their scope in the last month. If so, it's not a bad tactic. You know the old advice—don't put all your eggs in one basket. What they should do is spread their weapons caches around, so that if one sector gets too hot, they've got relief elsewhere. But you probably know more about secret rebel bases in these parts than I do."

Brent couldn't decide if that was meant to be a question or a complaint. He decided to pass on it with a noncommittal grunt. Then he said, "So what you're basically saying is that this area has become more of a playing field. Has that caused you any problems?"

Horton snorted derisively. "When is this job ever without problems? Oh, it's a bit harder to snoop around, but as long as I'm within striking distance of this river, no one seems to get too nervous. They figure I'm working on the dam project. But I suppose I wouldn't want to be in these parts without an official-looking pass. A lot of the troops are unsophisticated. They're just peasants who had the bad fortune to get conscripted. Too literal and simplistic for my tastes. They hear the word 'American' and they automatically think 'enemy.' But downtown in the big city, they're a bit more cool. They're equal-opportunity users. They don't care where you come from as long as they can get something useful out of you.''

Brent resisted asking if they had gotten anything useful out of Horton in addition to engineering advice. Instead, he stole a glance at his watch. He was anxious to start working on the defective computer program, which could take hours to analyze. ''Speaking of getting something useful,'' he said, ''I think that you have some bad disks for me to work on, right? Maybe we'd better get going on that business.''

Horton nodded, and they turned and began to walk toward his trailer. ''Right. Now here's the problem your company's software has caused me. . . .''

It took Brent two hours of detailed work to solve the problem, a tendency for one of the programs to take documents and reduce them to meaningless symbols without warning. The source of the problem turned out to be a power surge a week ago that had fried a sector of the disk. Normally, Brent would have simply exchanged a new program for the damaged one in this situation, but Horton insisted on recovering right away some files that had been reduced to an illegible jumble. Using all his skill, and patching together compatible features from several different recovery programs, Brent was finally able to bring them back to life.

Predictably, Horton wasn't even gracious enough to say thanks. He seemed to think that the problem wouldn't have occurred in the first place if the disks had been perfect. Brent made an attempt to explain the effects of electrical back surges on disks that were far more delicate than they looked, but he gave up after a few minutes. Horton didn't want his opinion to be confused by facts.

After grabbing something to eat in the workers' mess hall, Brent piled into his Rover and sped away. It would have been nice to spend the night in a decent bed, but the price would have included listening to more of Horton's dogmatic monologues.

Brent had been particularly uneasy in Horton's presence. Of all the interviews that he had conducted with stringers and agents so far, he found the one with Horton the most disturbing. The man's attitude seemed to be off center. There was something about him that Brent didn't like and didn't trust. Horton would definitely merit a lot of extra investigation. Brent would make that clear in his next report.

Brent headed in the direction of Addis Ababa after leaving Horton. There were no more agents or stringers left in this isolated region to check, and the rest of the names on Brent's list were either back in the capital city or north of it. But as he drove along, he caught sight of several different plumes of smoke in the distance. They reminded him of what Horton had said about roving bands of troops, unsophisticated troops who had a chip on their shoulders about Americans. Brent couldn't help thinking about Melissa Carlson, encamped there all by herself. If the word was out, mistaken or not, that she was engaged in espionage, she would be a very tempting target. She was certainly vulnerable, and as far as he knew, she was weaponless.

The more he thought about Melissa and her isolation, the more uneasy he got. He was still sensitive about the fact that Chelga had died in the middle of his investigative interview. For all he knew, anyone he visited might be in special danger. All his movements might be under surveillance. Even though he had been particularly cautious, he knew that a team of experienced trackers, with a combination of skill and good luck, could follow anyone without the quarry's being aware of it. For this reason, and because there was no one else around likely to watch out for Melissa, Brent began to feel the heavy weight of responsibility, which sat like a lump in his stomach.

Finally, he slowed the Rover to a crawl and swung around in a tight turn. The least he could do was to check on Melissa and warn her that the political situation in her region was heating up. The decision made him feel better immediately. He was looking forward to seeing her again.

By the time he had driven to within a mile of Melissa's camp, Brent knew that there was serious trouble. Several sets of tire tracks that hadn't been there this morning were in evidence along the road. But much more frightening was the pillar of smoke rising dead ahead.

His jaw tightly set, Brent pulled over to the side of the road behind the cover of some trees and grabbed a wrench from the tool kit. He stepped out of the vehicle and slid under the Rover on his back, maneuvering until he was right under the hollow compartment in front of the gas tank. The nuts were tight, but he exerted a steady counterclockwise force until they turned and loosened. Then he removed them quickly, spinning them to a blur with the tip of his forefinger.

When all six nuts had been removed, he allowed the flat metal cover to drop down into his hands. After setting it on the ground beside him, he reached up and released the disassembled Colt AR–15 from its padded mounts and set it next to his right hip. Then he pulled down all the rounds of ammunition, dropping the clips next to the AR–15. Finally, he replaced the cover on the compartment, but he didn't fasten the nuts as tight as they had been.

He scooted out from under the Rover. Sitting now, his back against the car, he quickly assembled the automatic weapon and slapped a clip into place. Cradling the weapon in his right hand, he eased himself to his feet, constantly sweeping his eyes back and forth. There was no one in sight, and no unexplained motion. He knelt down and retrieved the wrench and the remaining ammo clips. He tossed them into the front seat and followed them in, careful not to slam the door. Then he eased the Rover into first gear and began to creep down the road toward Melissa's encampment.

As he drew closer, an acrid odor assaulted his nostrils. It smelled like a combination of burning gasoline and rubber. If memory was any indicator, that had to be a burning car. When he came over the final rise and at last had a clear view and a clear shot, he stopped the Rover and stuffed some extra clips into his pockets. Then he opened the door noiselessly and slipped to the ground. Using a zigzag pattern, he ran behind the nearest tree and reconnoitered the area.

The column of smoke was, indeed, rising from Melissa's car, once a red Blazer. What was left of it was sooty and blackened. To make it burn that thoroughly, someone must have doused it liberally with cans of gasoline or some other accelerant. Its own gas tank, of course, would have added fuel to the fire.

Brent's eyes swept the small compound. Melissa's three large tents, one to live in and two for storage, were lying flat on the ground. It looked as if they had been slashed and ripped as well as knocked over. The three crates that had been neatly stacked outside one of the supply tents had been smashed open and their contents scattered about. The result was a jumble of splintered wood, torn books, broken dishes, and trampled articles of clothing.

There was no sign of Melissa herself, and Brent wasn't sure whether that was a relief or a source of new worry. Then an inner voice told him that she would be better off dead than in the custody of troops so undisciplined. He pushed the thought aside roughly.

Under the collapsed tents, there were a few lumpy forms. They would probably turn out to be cots or foot-lockers or something of the sort, but he felt compelled to check on them anyway. He waited a full three minutes before moving from behind his cover. In that time, there was no sound other than the sighing of the wind, and no motion other than the mournful sway of the long grass. Finally, he broke cover and moved toward the collapsed tents.

He examined the lumps under the first tent. It had been one of the storage tents, and nothing that he felt through the nylon material had the resiliency or the shape of a human body. He moved to the middle tent, which had been Melissa's living quarters. He walked around the collapsed pile of material until he came to the entrance flap. He had better look inside this one.

He lifted one side of the flap with his left hand, pulling a portion of the tent a couple of feet off the ground. Before sticking his head inside, he sniffed the air cautiously, then breathed a sigh of relief. There was no sign of putrefaction. Still, he had better check on the interior. But just as he was about to poke his head through the zippered opening, he heard the sound of footsteps behind him.

In one instinctive motion, his left hand dropped the tent flap and swung over to support the barrel of the Colt. Simultaneously, he squatted and spun round to face the source of the noise, raising the weapon to belt level. His right index finger poised expectantly around the trigger.

At that moment, the gun became a living extension of himself. It was now the focused outer envelope of his vision and his reflexes and his aim. Hundreds of hours of practice had brought him to this crucial instant when the merest squeeze of a finger would spew forth instant and certain death. And those same hundreds of hours of practice now enabled him to halt the twitch of his finger, swing the silent barrel harmlessly toward the ground, and lay the weapon down on the grass.

It was Melissa. She had emerged from her hiding place in the brush and brambles around her devastated camp and was running toward him. She ran straight into his arms and buried her face in his chest. Instantly, she broke into tears. It was the breaking of the floodgates of fear and relief. Her heaving sobs tore at his heart, but he realized that it was something that she must do or burst into a million pieces. So he simply held her tightly and whispered soothing words.

Eventually, the racking sobs gave way to slight shudders, and soon all was reduced to sniffles. Melissa looked up into his eyes and then looked quickly down again. "Oh, no, I must look just awful," she murmured.

Brent placed his hand under her chin and gently tilted

her head back up. "You look wonderful to me," he said. "I can't tell you how wonderful." Their eyes held for a moment, and then he leaned down and gently kissed her. Tears formed again in her eyes, but he knew that her nightmare of fear had passed.

She pulled back slightly to look at his face. "I can't tell you how happy I am to see you."

"It's all right. No one is going to hurt you." He found himself stroking her hair. "Do you feel up to telling me what happened? Are you hurt in any way?"

"No, I'm okay. Well, aside from some scratches that I got from those brambles over there. I guess you could say I was lucky." Her eyes filled up with tears again as she surveyed the havoc wreaked upon her belongings. "But I don't feel so lucky."

"Don't worry about that now. We'll deal with this mess later. But it would really help me to know what happened."

She stepped back and folded her arms in anger and frustration. "What happened was that a pack of animals destroyed a year and a half of my hard work. No—that's not fair to animals! They don't act like that!" She looked sheepishly at him. "I'm sorry. I don't normally carry on like this."

"Hey, you have a right to be angry. They did a terrible thing. But do you know *why* they did it? Did anyone say anything to you, threaten you?"

"No. I wasn't even here at the time, thank God. I was out with the pack. But I heard all this commotion in the distance. And then there was all that dense black smoke and a sound like a muffled explosion." She focused her gaze in the distance, reliving the memories. "And so I left the pack and started back, half running and half walking. It must have taken me three-quarters of an hour. They were pulling away when I got close enough to see—"

"Who was pulling away? What were they driving?"

"They were soldiers, I guess. At least, they were all dressed in khaki shirts and shorts. And they were driving jeeps—four jeeps, I think."

"How many troops were there?"

"I'd have to guess. I think there were two or three men in each jeep."

"So there may have been from eight to twelve of them. And did they have guns?"

"Yes! The last thing they did was drive around in circles, shooting insanely into my tents." Suddenly, the color left her face and her voice dropped to a barely audible whisper: "I could have been in one of those tents."

Brent pulled her to him and wrapped his arms tightly around her. "Yes, you could have been—but you weren't. Hang on to that thought. You're alive and unharmed, and that's all that counts."

She looked around with apprehension. "What happens if they come back? Do you think they'll come back?"

Brent looked thoughtful. "I won't lie to you, Melissa. I think there's a good chance that they will come back. But when they do, we'll be long gone." He glanced quickly around the compound. Long shadows were beginning to form as the late-afternoon sun moved down toward the horizon. "Look, let's take a couple of minutes to grab your most important stuff, including some clothes.

We can put them in the back of my Rover. Then, I suggest that we put some distance between us and this place."

Melissa looked stricken. "But I can't just go off and leave the rest of my things."

"That's exactly what you're going to have to do. But I think that your property—what's left of it—will be safe for now. Those men weren't just looters. They were probably looking for some documents. Or, let's be blunt, they may have been looking for you. They tossed your things to leave a message."

Melissa looked confused. "Why on earth would they be looking for me?"

Brent's eyes again swept the horizon apprehensively. "Let's start gathering up a few of your things. I'll explain what I know as soon as we're on our way to safety." He saw where her curious gaze was fixed. "Yes, including an explanation of that gun and how I came to have it."

Chapter Five

They had traveled north through the moon-dappled hours of the night, changing places at the wheel every hour. To reduce their chances of being seen, Brent had kept the headlights switched off as much as possible, which meant that the journey had taken almost twice as much time as in daylight. It also meant a serious strain on the eyes as they crawled along severely substandard roads. But Brent's immediate concern was to get Melissa to safety, and he believed in taking the conservative approach when civilians were involved.

At the optimum, though he had not yet broached the subject with Melissa, that meant getting her on a flight out of the country immediately. At the minimum, it meant getting her back to the relative safety of Addis Ababa, where a more tolerant attitude toward foreigners seemed to prevail. And there, the college community with which she was affiliated would surely offer a temporary haven until he could figure out a plan of action.

For the last half hour, the road had skirted the edge of the Awash River valley. According to the odometer, they had traveled about a hundred and eighty miles in just under five hours. That certainly wouldn't win any races, but they hadn't seen one soldier or one military vehicle in all that time. Brent was positive that they had left far behind the troops who had trashed Melissa's camp.

He looked over at her. She was dozing, her head resting on a rolled-up sweatshirt wedged against the passenger door. He smiled. She was certainly pleasant company. And she was definitely someone who seemed trustworthy. It was a feeling that he hadn't savored in quite some time.

Though she had been surprised earlier to learn of his real occupation, she had absorbed the information with a minimum of fuss. She had quickly grasped the situation and accepted the facts that he had felt free to relay to her. About some things, of course, she was still in the dark.

He turned his attention back to the road. The light was changing. Dawn was gearing itself up for another workday, and twenty minutes later, its subtle glow softly dominated the scene. Straight ahead, slightly to the left of the road, was a rock formation, its three rounded peaks looking like a miniature mountain range even though the highest one rose no more than forty feet. Brent felt tired and gritty and hungry, and now that they were out of the danger zone, a short stopover wouldn't hurt. And those rocks could act as a lookout point. Climbing them would even serve to limber up some stiff muscles. He eased off the road and drove toward the formation.

Melissa sensed the change. She opened her eyes, stretched, and looked around. "What is it? Is there a problem?"

"No, everything's fine. It's just that I could stand to move around a bit. And have something to eat."

"Um, that sounds good to me too."

Straight ahead, a fissure in the rock was just large enough to conceal the Rover, and he eased the vehicle around in a half circle and then backed it in gingerly. He told Melissa, "I'll have to get out on your side. It's a bit tight over here by my door. But it gets us nicely out of sight."

He scooted over and followed her out of the passenger's door, grabbing his binoculars as he exited. The sound of steady, distant thunder made him look up at the sky, but no rain clouds were visible. It was puzzling. After bending and stretching luxuriously for a minute, he leaned back against the Rover and looked up at the rock formation looming over them. It looked like an easy trek to the top. "What about it—do you want to climb up with me?" he asked her. "I want to look around and see what's going on, behind us and in front of us."

She looked it over with a practiced eye. "Sure. Piece of cake." Before he could offer any advice, she was already ascending. He watched admiringly. She didn't need his advice about climbing at all. She had been tutored well—maybe by her jackals.

When they reached the top ten minutes later, they first looked east across the valley at the undulating highlands whose purple shadows were now streaked by the early-morning light. In the distance, bare and craggy peaks cut a jagged line across the horizon. Closer, and lower, sparsely green hills rose and fell in an unbroken line from north to south. And just across the road, at the bottom of a precipitous gorge, flowed the Awash River. They could not see the river itself from where they stood, because of the depth of its valley, but they could see the top of a waterfall about a quarter of a mile to their left. Brent now understood the distant thunder that had caught his attention before.

He turned in a slow pivot, scanning the surrounding terrain for any signs of activity. To the west was a scrubland plain with bushes and sparse vegetation clinging precariously to rocky surfaces. Running north and south were dramatic highland mountains that seemed to stand sentinel over the Awash River. But in all directions, there was no sign of human activity.

Melissa broke the silence: "It's just gorgeous, isn't it?"

Brent nodded as he examined a distant set of shadows through the binoculars for the second time, just to be sure.

She went on: "And just think—all this beauty is the product of enormous destruction."

Brent lowered the binoculars and turned to look at her. "Destruction? What do you mean?"

"Well, this is all part of the Great Rift, you know." Melissa's hand swept from horizon to horizon. "Deep under our feet, the continental plates are drifting apart. Their sliding and stretching produces fractures and tilts, even domes of hot lava that shove everything up and out of their way."

"It sounds like a recipe for an earthquake or an eruption." Brent looked at the distant peaks suspiciously, noticing that some of them were, indeed, cone-shaped.

"Good observation. Earthquakes are a frequent occurrence in these parts. Luckily, unlike in California, the population isn't very dense around here.'' She pointed to the north. ''And as for volcanoes, just look at all those black outcroppings of rock.''

''Lava formations?''

''Give the man an A plus. That's exactly what they are. So all these subterranean forces are heaving and buckling and collapsing the earth's crust. They've destroyed the smooth exterior surface. But without them, we wouldn't have this marvelous landscape.''

Brent caught himself looking at the surface on which he stood. ''You know, suddenly the ground doesn't feel so solid anymore.''

Melissa laughed. ''It never was and never will be. It's just that it's normally such an extended process that we humans never notice it. Except here along the Great Rift. Here we're in a very active place, geologically speaking. Dramatic effects can be detected in just a few decades— even years, sometimes.''

''Well, it looks like the only dramatic effects we're likely to see this morning will come from Mother Earth. I don't see any sign of troop activity at all.'' He glanced at his watch. ''In fact, they're probably just getting up.''

''That's fine with me.'' She shuddered. ''I had enough dramatic effects yesterday to last a lifetime.''

''Today's going to be different. Now that we're so far from the Lake Abaya region, I think it's perfectly safe to travel by daylight again, and I figure that it'll take no more than two hours to reach Addis Ababa from here. We're just about home free.''

Melissa smiled at the thought, then looked down in annoyance as her stomach growled. ''Say, didn't you mention something about a bite to eat? I'm embarrassed to tell you that I'm getting some impatient messages here.''

''Sure did. I'm afraid that I can't offer you a traditional breakfast, but I've got the makings for some sandwiches.''

''I'll be grateful for anything at all. I'm famished!''

Brent pointed in the direction of the Rover. ''Breakfast awaits us. Shall we?''

They descended in a zigzag fashion, carefully choosing surfaces free of rock chips and other hazards to solid footing. When they reached the Rover, Brent looked at Melissa inquiringly. ''Say, how about eating across the road there on the edge of the cliff? I wouldn't mind getting a closer look at that waterfall. Should be picturesque.''

''I'd like that. I've spent enough time sitting in the Rover.''

''Amen to that.'' He crawled back through the passenger door and set about making sandwiches. He stuffed them and some bottles of mineral water into an orange backpack and emerged once again. He slung the backpack over his shoulders and offered Melissa his arm, saying, ''Let's see if we can find some grass and turn this into a real picnic.''

''I wouldn't bet on grass in this terrain. But we might find a big patch of moss if we're lucky.'' She pointed to a boulder about the size of a minivan. ''Let's head for that rock near the edge. It should have some moss at its base.''

''You're the nature expert. Lead on.''

In just a few minutes, they were standing on the edge of the precipice, staring in fascination at the thundering waterfall across the way and a quarter of a mile down-

stream. She told him that it was the product of several
tributaries that, obeying the law of gravity, flowed down
through the highlands until they came to the Awash River.
Hundreds of thousands of years ago, the Awash would
have been waiting at the higher level where they now
stood, and the tributaries would have joined it less spec-
tacularly. But now, thanks to powerful erosion and the
rifting of which she had spoken before, the tributaries
had to engage in a diving free-fall to join the Awash River
in its valley below.

Because the sides of the valley narrowed as they con-
verged toward the bottom, the falls were forced to flow
in a series of steps, three in all. It reminded Brent of his
boyhood Slinky, a toy that sinuously flowed down stairs
or an inclined plane in a series of looping movements.
First, the falls poured over the lip of the valley and
dropped straight down for fifty yards. Then they splattered
against an outcropping of rock, gathered in a shimmering
pool, and fell again. Finally, about twenty yards from
the bottom, they collided with another ledge before pooling one last time and then splashing down into the Awash
in a glistening veil.

Brent and Melissa viewed the spectacle in silence for
several minutes, charting the progress of the shifting rain-
bows that danced among the waters, and periodically
feeling a fine mist against their faces. The river was only
about forty feet wide at this point, having narrowed considerably about a mile upstream, so the water flowed and
rippled below them in a constant rush. In addition, there
was the turbulence caused by thousands of gallons per
minute being dumped into the river by the waterfall.
Large bubbles formed and burst almost faster than the

eye could detect. Swirls of froth formed everchanging patterns on the dark surface of the water. Floating branches whirled in dizzying patterns as they were caught up in small, foaming eddies and then ejected by the waterfall to continue their journey downstream.

Adding to the mixture of eye-catching motions were the antics of the birds. Melissa identified them as chestnut-winged starlings, and their graceful flight was a treat to behold. At times, like oversized hummingbirds, they seemed to be suspended in place, riding the turbulent air currents. Then they would break away by folding their wings to their sides and plummeting to the surface of the river as if they were about to drown. At the last second, they would pull up, skim the surface of the water, and then soar back into midair to be caught again by the sustaining currents of air.

After watching the swooping and skimming for a few minutes, Melissa leaned over to speak above the roar of the falls about something in the starlings' behavior that was puzzling her: "Brent, have you noticed how some of those birds disappear from time to time?"

He nodded vigorously, and spoke close to her ear: "You mean behind the waterfall? Yes. I'm glad you spotted it too. I thought it was just an optical illusion— or a sign that I needed glasses!"

As they watched, it happened again. A pair of starlings in formation, side by side, rose into the air, traced a sweeping curve to the right side of the waterfall, and seemed to disappear into the curtain of water. It was as if they had carried out a suicide pact, for there was no way that they would not be beaten down and crushed by the force of the falling water. But then, a few minutes later, two starlings suddenly darted back out from the right side of the waterfall and rejoined the rest of the throng. There was no way to tell if this was the same pair, but it was now obvious that birds were slipping behind the waterfall with relative ease.

Melissa cupped her hands and spoke into Brent's ear: "You know something? That sure looks like chick-feeding behavior to me. I think there are nests behind that waterfall. There must be a significant gap back there, probably a formation of ledges or crevices."

Brent nodded his understanding. Even though animal behavior was Melissa's specialty and not his, that seemed like a logical explanation to him too. Reluctantly, he broke the spell and said, "Well, I can't think of a more picturesque place to have breakfast. What about you?"

She started to agree, but stopped suddenly before saying a word. She turned and looked up the road, her brow furrowed in concentration. Then she looked at Brent, concern etched on her face.

He grabbed her arm. "Right. I heard it too. Somebody's driving this way from the north. It can't be the crew from back there in Lake Abaya, but let's not take any chances until we see who it is." He looked around hurriedly, gauging their distance from the Rover. There probably wasn't enough time to get back to it. Besides, he wouldn't want to lead anyone to its precarious hiding place. "Get behind this boulder," he snapped. "Keep it between you and whoever that is."

Together, they scooted behind the boulder and crouched down. In spite of the noise from the waterfall, the sounds of a labored engine steadily grew louder. Peering carefully from behind the rock, Brent watched as an old flatbed truck rounded a bend about a hundred yards away and then bucked and sputtered to a halt. The driver emerged from the stalled vehicle and kicked viciously at a tire. Half a dozen men dropped off the back of the flatbed and ambled forward toward the driver, complaining in a language that Brent did not understand. He groaned inwardly and cursed his luck. All the men were dressed in identical khaki shirts and shorts.

He ducked back down and reported to Melissa in a loud whisper: "Soldiers, and they're having engine trouble. They haven't seen us yet."

Melissa turned a stricken look upon him. "What are we going to do?"

"We can't stay here. They're likely to stretch their legs while somebody works on the engine." He looked over his shoulder. "Down looks like the only way. Hang on a minute."

He dropped to his hands and knees and scrambled backward to the edge of the cliff, careful to keep the boulder squarely between him and the troops. When he reached the very edge, he glanced over and down, and breathed a sigh of relief. Finally, a break. The slope on this side was much less precipitous than its counterpart across the way. He could even make out the trace of a path snaking its way to the bottom. It looked as if generations of use had stamped out a trail of sorts, though for what reason he had no idea.

Melissa was watching him avidly. He signaled for her to join him, and watched as she crawled rapidly toward him on her hands and knees. When she reached him, he wasted no time, and sat on the edge and slipped down over the side. Turning, he reached back up and offered

Melissa his hand as support. "Quick! Down here!" She half stepped and half slid over the lip of the canyon and crouched out of sight next to him. Brent eased back around her and pulled himself up with his hands until he was eye level with the surface. He could see a couple of the soldiers as they wandered around, looking bored, but there was no sign of alarm. Melissa and he had not been spotted.

He dropped back down quietly and stepped in front of Melissa again. He brought his mouth close to her ear. "This is a bit treacherous, loose stones and all. Let me go first. Just watch your footing." Impulsively, he kissed her lightly on the temple, and then turned and led the way.

The trail was fairly steep and littered with stone fragments, but it looked just wide enough to support a pack animal, and so it did not seem overly precarious. But the number of insect bites increased as they descended, adding to the discomfort level. In only fifteen minutes, they were at the bottom, the sound of the falls thundering in their ears.

Brent leaned toward Melissa and said, "Let's stay as close as possible to this cliff." He pointed back up. "It'll make it harder for them to see us if they look down at the river."

Melissa stood on tiptoe to reach his ear. "Shouldn't we move away from this trail a bit?"

Brent nodded. It wouldn't be a bad idea at all, since the trail formed a line of sight that the eye naturally followed. He pointed back upstream. "That way, away from the waterfall."

Melissa cupped her hand around her ear to show that

she had missed the last part. Brent leaned closer. "Away from the falls. Toward the falls is the direction they'll be looking in."

Melissa nodded her understanding. It was obvious that there wouldn't be much comfortable conversation at this sustained volume. They began to move upstream, away from the falls. It was very slow going, because the base of the cliff was littered with fallen rocks, but to walk on the clearer surface next to the river would have exposed them to plain view from above.

They had worked their way about ten yards upstream, slipping and sliding on the uneven jumble of rocks, when Brent felt a sting on top of his head, and then another. He reached up instinctively with a swatting motion. But even as he reached, part of his brain registered the fact that it was no insect. The flinty stings increased, and he could feel more chips pelting his scalp. From the corner of his eye, he saw Melissa reach up in confusion to protect the top of her head too.

Brent craned his neck upward to see what on earth was going on. As he searched, he had to look through protectively extended fingers, for now the chips were increasing in size and frequency. His heart froze at what he saw.

High above, but tumbling rapidly, a cloud of dust and debris was bouncing down the slope above them. That was bad enough, but what came after it was worse. The dust was simply a prelude to a barrage of falling rocks and boulders. It looked as if half the slope were plummeting—and it was heading straight for them.

Brent grabbed Melissa by the waist and pushed her up against the side of the gorge under a small shelflike outcrop. Then he wrapped his arm around her shoulders and drew her close to his side. They flattened themselves against the rock wall, hugging the unyielding surface for dear life. There was nothing more to do except wait and pray.

At first, the noise of the waterfall drowned out the sound of falling pebbles and stones. Then, as the rate of debris increased, a pattering sound behind them began to intrude. As the rockslide advanced, the pattering sound changed to a clatter. It reminded Brent of the onslaught of a sudden shower, where initial, gentle drops quickly give way to pelting rain. But in this case, what was falling was far more lethal than rain.

As the dust in the air increased and as the sound intensified to deep, hollow thuds and sharp crashes, they hugged the base of the slope even more tightly. The bone-jarring vibrations from tons of rocks and boulders smashing violently into the ground around them communicated itself through the soles of their boots. The ground danced crazily beneath their feet. The very rock face against which they were pressing their faces seemed to hum in sympathetic harmony. They could feel occasional small rock splinters grazing the backs of their legs as rock crashed against rock and sent chips flying. But the declivity of the gorge and the slight lip of rock over their heads prevented any of the boulders from hitting them directly.

And then, even though the dust surrounding them was thicker than ever, they suddenly became aware that the thundering sound of the waterfall was dominating again. The pounding and dumping sound had retreated. Tentatively, Brent extended his right hand out and behind him, palm upward. He felt a flick or two, but the deadly hail had come to an abrupt halt.

He turned and took Melissa even more tightly into the shelter of his arms. They stood there for a moment, locked in a heartfelt embrace that was part relief and part a prayer of thanksgiving. Then they slowly separated and turned to view the damage.

They stumbled awkwardly as they turned, feet sliding on the loose chips and pebbles that had not been there just minutes before. A few yards away, roughly halfway between them and the riverbank, there now rose a rounded hump of boulders about six feet high. Shallower piles of decreasingly smaller rocks radiated in all directions with the mound as center. At the outer circumference, stones and chips flared out in a raggedly circular pattern, as if they had been hastily arranged by an amateur landscaper. If Brent and Melissa had been walking a few feet closer to the river, that mound would now be their tombstone.

Melissa looked up worriedly into Brent's eyes. ''Are you all right? Did you get hurt?''

''I'm fine. But what about you?''

She extended her right leg to the side and looked at the back of her white cotton sock. She let the leg of the jeans fall back in place. ''I felt some stones banging against my legs. They really stung, but I don't see any bloodstains. So I guess I'm okay.'' She shivered slightly. ''What was that all about—an earthquake?''

He shook his head. ''I don't think so. The rockslide was confined to one narrow strip. If that was an earthquake, you'd expect rocks to have fallen all up and down the gorge. No, I'm afraid it was our friends up there.''

Melissa blanched. ''Do you think they've seen us?''

"I'm not sure. If we're lucky, they could have been just entertaining themselves by tossing rocks down the slope. That could have started a landslide. But I'd better check instead of just guessing. Stay here under this ledge. I'm going to see what's going on."

"Be careful!"

He eased out slowly, trying to get just a glimpse of the ridge above them without exposing himself to any observers. Nobody was in sight. But even as he watched, two soldiers slid over the edge, eased their feet onto the trail head, and began to descend. They held no weapons, so Brent assumed that they were simply killing time, not stalking them. Their backs would be to him and Melissa while they were descending the trail, but if they turned, they would surely see them. And when they reached the bottom, there would be an inevitable encounter.

Brent moved back to Melissa's side. "Trouble," he whispered. "Two of them are coming down, but they haven't seen us yet." His mind raced for a solution. It didn't look good. He had left his Colt in the car and the Rover was inaccessible until the troops moved on. Melissa and he could continue their slow progress upstream along the rock-strewn banks of the river, but they couldn't hope to outdistance troops moving on the road above. And now there would be two soldiers right behind them every step of the way. There seemed to be no way out. They were trapped.

Chapter Six

As he surveyed the seemingly impossible situation, Brent's eye suddenly fell on the swift torrent of the river that was racing by them. It would take a powerful swimmer, and even then . . . . But there was no other option. "Melissa, can you swim?" he asked.

She looked at the swift current with widened eyes. "Yes, but . . . ."

"I'm afraid it's our only chance." He put a hand on her shoulder and pointed with the other one. "See that pile of debris on the bank up that way? If we're lucky, we might be able to find a log or a branch big enough to support us. This is one heck of a current and I'd sure feel better if I had a homemade life preserver."

Melissa agreed, and together they broke into a loping run, careful not to twist an ankle on the loose rocks. As they ran the obstacle course, they glanced back over their shoulders to see what the soldiers were doing. The two men had stopped about one-third of the way down the slope, and one of them was gesturing wildly in their direction.

Brent and Melissa scrambled and leapfrogged over rocks until they reached the pile of driftwood, where they stood for a moment, hands on hips, breathing deeply. Then Brent reached down and tugged at a gnarled log resting in the water but wedged into the side of the riverbank. A branch extending from the log was caught in some rushes, but he felt some give as he pushed and pulled it. He looked up at Melissa and said with a smile, "I think we've got us a life raft."

She turned and looked up to the top of the gorge. Four soldiers were squatting on the lip of the precipice, watching them curiously. "Those two have managed to alert the rest of the squad." She raised her arms in frustration. "Will we ever lose them?"

Brent pointed to the log at his feet. "When we get this thing moving, we sure will. There's no way that they can keep up with the current on foot, and they've got a stalled truck. If we can paddle ourselves out to the middle, we should shoot downstream like an express train, and we won't bail out until we're certain that they're far behind. Then we can figure out what comes next."

Melissa sat on a rock and began removing her hiking boots and padded socks. "I'd just as soon stay dry, of course, but our friends up there aren't cooperating." She thought for a moment, then pulled off her sweatshirt.

Brent sat on the ground next to her and began removing his own boots. When he saw her tie her shoelaces together and drape the boots around her neck, he indicated the backpack at his feet. "Stuff them in here. We can secure the pack to the log." He pointed to the rushing water. "I wouldn't bet on being able to hang on to our boots if they're just dangling from our necks, and we're going to need them when we bail out.''

"Good idea. I'll take the sweatshirt too, if there's room.''

"No problem. It'll go in here on top of the boots.'' He looked at the swift current and noted the branches and other debris being swept along on its surface. Though his shirt and trousers would weigh him down when they got soaked, they would act as protection against the certainty of scratches and abrasions. Besides, even with water-soaked clothing, he would have the buoyant log for support.

Having zippered all the compartments of the backpack securely, Brent dropped it on the ground and set to work freeing the log. He sat on the bank and pushed at the log with his feet. When he felt it begin to tear itself away from the tangle of reeds and branches, he grunted in satisfaction.

He turned and looked back up at the ridge. The troops were all standing now, and even from a distance they appeared to be agitated. They had finally figured out what Brent and Melissa were about to do, and they didn't seem very pleased.

"Melissa, hand me the backpack.'' Brent reached back, snared a dangling strap, and set to work securing it to the log. He didn't want it to hang too loosely, but tying it too tightly might cause problems later if they had to abandon the log quickly. Finally, satisfied that he had it just right, he stood up and approached Melissa. He took her in his arms and looked into her eyes. "Well, kiddo, time to get wet.'' He leaned down and nuzzled his cheek against hers. "Look, I want to tell you . . . I mean, what I feel is . . . ."

"I know, Brent, I know. I feel exactly the same way."

They clung to each other tightly, reluctant to pull apart. A sudden report from overhead caused Brent to jerk his head up. He was in time to see a puff of smoke emerging from the rifle that one of the soldiers was aiming at them. A splash in the river behind them caused Brent to jerk his head back in that direction.

"Brent, they're shooting at us!" Melissa cried.

"Quick—into the river!"

They scrambled to the river's edge and plunged in feet first, one on each side of the log. Brent was shocked to feel the pull of the current. It was enormously powerful, more than he had expected. He pulled himself up and looked over the top of the bobbing log. He was relieved to see that Melissa had snared a thick branch with both hands, but he could tell that she had to exert great effort to hold on. He reached back underwater with his feet and shoved mightily at the bank of the river in an effort to free the log.

With a shudder, the log finally tore loose and plunged into the furious current. At first, the acceleration was frightening. It had the stomach-churning kick of an unexpectedly powerful sports car. Then a breathtaking, exhilarating feeling took over. The experience matched any amusement park ride that Brent had ever encountered.

The smack of a bullet in the log close to his head sobered him in a second. He could feel chips of bark spattering painfully against the side of his face. Luckily, Melissa was on the side of the log away from the soldiers, and she would be safe from their gunfire. But if their accuracy increased, he was in mortal danger.

The deafening sound of pounding water increased as the log to which they were desperately clinging approached the waterfall. Brent strained to turn his head enough to see the soldiers lined up at the top of the ridge. Though he could hear nothing above the thunder of the waterfall's torrent, he could see puffs of smoke emerging from the barrels of their rifles. They were laying down a deadly pattern of fire, and the number of bullets thudding into the log was increasing second by second.

Fearful for Melissa's safety, Brent pulled himself up until he could see the top of her head. Relief flooded over him. She was still hanging on gamely. As he began to lower himself again, a painful burning sensation flared up in his left earlobe. Instinctively, he let go of the log with his left hand and reached for his ear.

With only one hand supporting him, he was no match for the force of the current. It whipped him around, slamming his shoulders brutally against the roughness of the log. He felt his right hand losing its grip, and almost before he had time to complete a deep breath, he had been pulled beneath the surface.

The underwater turbulence spun him end over end and from side to side. He felt as helpless and as limp as a piece of laundry in a washing machine. He didn't even try to swim. It would have been a futile gesture. He simply gave himself up to the sweep and whirl of the current and prayed that he could hold his breath long enough to reach a handhold of some kind.

Now he could feel the bone-jarring pounding of the waterfall on the surface above him reverberating through his quivering body. Opening his eyes to mere slits, he could see, even in the murk and gloom, thousands of bubbles dancing crazily all around him as he spun in concert with them. And he could hear the muted but all-pervasive thunderous sound that enveloped him as completely as the water itself.

The painful pressure in his chest and the shuddering urge to take a breath told him that his time had almost run out. Unless he could reach the surface quickly, he was finished. He reached out with his arms and flailed them out and around in a butterfly stroke. He didn't know if he was facing up or down, but he had to make one last, desperate effort.

Suddenly, the bubbles disappeared and the pounding sensation grew far less intense. Brent had the sensation of rising, of being squirted upward like a cork, and he assisted the apparent motion with his hands and his feet. When his head and his shoulders unexpectedly broke the surface of the water, his huge, gulping breath was the sweetest of his entire life.

Now the waterfall was again an intense, unbearable roar instead of a dull, underwater rumble. He looked around as he paddled in place. Behind him was an impenetrable sheet of water. In front of him was the uneven, sloping surface of moss-covered rock. The churning action of the falling water was pushing him insistently toward the rock even as he attempted to dog-paddle in place. He had emerged behind the waterfall.

As his leg banged against the underwater surface of the cliff, he reached out and grabbed an outcrop of rock located just above the surface of the water at eye level. He could feel the lower part of his body continuing to drift to the left as the current attempted to pull him to the outer edge of the waterfall. The last thing that he needed was to be swept out the side and back around to the front of the waterfall where he could again become the object of target practice for the soldiers. He grasped his handhold even more tightly.

Thinking of target practice, he reached gingerly toward his left ear. When he drew back his hand and examined it, he found his fingers streaked with blood. He cupped his hand and dipped it into the water. Then, tilting his head to the side, he gently rinsed off his ear several times.

Expending his small reserves of energy, Brent pulled himself slowly and painfully out of the water and onto a small, sloping shelf of rock. Battered and exhausted, and fighting off a wave of nausea, he rolled over on his back and covered his eyes with his right arm.

A faint, flapping sound nearby caused him to drop his arm and open his eyes. He had to work hard to focus; his eyes seemed to be working in slow motion. Just a few feet away, a pair of starlings were landing at the edge of a deep crevice and stuffing the gullets of several insatiable chicks with insects. Brent smiled as he recalled what Melissa had said about them.

As he sat up, he immediately experienced a wave of vertigo. Melissa! Desperately, he blinked and looked around, but there was no sign of Melissa or of the log here behind the waterfall. Had she seen him when he was forced to let go of the log? Had she tried to reach this waterfall, or had she hung on to the log, unaware of his predicament, and been swept downstream? He tried to hold off the unthinkable, but an image of Melissa struggling desperately and futilely underwater refused to go away.

The light began to dim and a fuzzy curtain dropped over his eyes. Gray spots swam in front of him like colorless leaves caught in a whirlpool. His head seemed to be swaying uncontrollably in a clockwise rotation while an unpleasant buzzing sound kept time like a metronome. He shook his head and began to reach up with his right hand to rub his eyes. Before it even got there, he lost consciousness and fell over heavily on his side.

The starlings looked at him curiously for a moment, and then resumed feeding their young.

When Brent opened his eyes, the light had shifted in a subtle but noticeable way. It was brighter, there was no doubt of that. He stood up warily and brushed his hands over his damp clothes. More clearheaded now, he quickly figured out that the depth of this gorge meant that full, direct sunlight fell upon the riverbed for but an hour or two at noon each day. The rest of the time, varying degrees of shadows and partial illumination were the norm. If the light was growing brighter, it meant that midday was approaching. And that meant that he had been unconscious for some time.

His eyes eagerly swept the surface of the water a few feet below him. Branches and other debris floated by and disappeared around both edges of the waterfall, but there was no sign of Melissa. In spite of the danger that might still be lurking out there in the form of those soldiers, he had to figure out a way to begin searching for her. He began to consider his options.

He could edge his way sideways along this rock ledge

and emerge from behind the waterfall. If he could achieve a clear line of sight, he might be able to see some distance downstream. At the very least, he could peer out surreptitiously to discover how many soldiers were still stationed on the opposite shore.

On the other hand, he could begin to work himself straight up the face of this cliff. All the soldiers were on the other side of the river. If he could stay behind the waterfall and reach the rim of the gorge on this side, he might be able to go for help, even without the Land Rover. At this time of the year, encampments of nomadic herdsmen were a frequent sight in the highlands.

Whichever course he chose, there was no time to lose. He decided to begin by testing his footing on the rock face. Bare feet have both advantages and disadvantages when trying to gain purchase in crevices and crannies, and he had better find out quickly which was going to predominate.

He began to angle upward toward the left edge of the waterfall. He chose his footholds carefully, avoiding sharp edges and small openings in favor of smooth weathered surfaces and wide fissures. He discovered that while boots would have permitted faster and more aggressive progress, bare feet allowed for more intimate contact with the cliff and a more secure placement of his soles. He told himself that it was akin to the choice between wearing gloves or using bare hands. In fact, he knew that he had no choice. His boots were in the backpack, and the backpack had been swept away with Melissa.

When he looked back down a few minutes later, he found that he had ascended about fifteen feet. His eyes swept the waterline once again, but he saw nothing that looked like Melissa. But then he focused on a deep shadow on the cliff face below him toward the middle of the waterfall. From a lower elevation, he hadn't been able to see it. It was sheltered by an outcrop that blended in with the face of the cliff. The shadow began to intrigue him, and the more that he stared at it, the more it looked like the mouth of a cave. He decided to work his way sideways and downward for a closer look at it. Though it was unlikely, he didn't want to take the chance that Melissa might have taken shelter in a cave while he was unconscious.

As he drew closer, step by careful step, it became clear that it was, indeed, a cave mouth and not just a shadow. Just before stepping down gingerly to the ledge in front of the cave opening, he suddenly realized that he was clinging to a large iron ring as a handhold. Odd. How did an iron ring get attached here? He looked at it carefully. There was a patina of rust on the outside rim of the ring. That made sense; the air here was humid. But the inside surface of the ring was clean and smooth, as if abraded by frequent use. *That* made no sense.

He stepped down to the ledge and stood quietly to the left side of the entrance, listening carefully. There was a tingle at the back of his neck that had nothing to do with the temperature of the air. He didn't quite know what was going on, but he was reluctant to enter the cave too quickly. There seemed to be an element of danger in the air. He decided to proceed with extreme caution. He reached down and picked up a couple of stones.

He edged closer to the entrance and reached around the corner with his right hand. Using a strong wrist action, he flung one of the stones into the cave. He heard it bounce against a rock wall and clatter against the rock floor. Then there was silence. He threw another stone with the same results. Partially satisfied, he worked his way slowly into the cave, keeping his profile low and narrow.

There was just enough light to allow him to see that he was in a small natural cave about the size of a walk-in closet. He had to stoop a bit to keep from brushing his head against the rock ceiling, so he figured its height at just under six feet. The two side walls were unbroken, but the back wall had a dark gaping hole about four feet high and three wide. It gave this small cave the look of an antechamber. Apparently, there was more to the cave yet to be seen.

If Melissa had been here, perhaps she had moved on to the interior of the cave. He approached the hole at the back of the cave and knelt down in front of it. Slowly and cautiously, moving on hands and knees, he extended his head and shoulders into the opening, and was surprised to feel a steady breeze on his face.

He hugged the left wall of the tunnel in an attempt to let the daylight behind him stream over his shoulder; he was startled to see a gleam from the interior. It wasn't the feral gleam from animal eyes. He realized that right away. It was the sort of gleam that reflects from shiny metal or glass. Curious, he crawled forward about two yards more and reached out tentatively with his right hand. He felt something cold and smooth and hard. He grasped it in his fingers and crawled backward until he was once more in the antechamber. He sat back on his haunches and stared at the object.

He could hardly believe his eyes—a Coleman lantern!

A good, old green Coleman lantern just like the one he had used in his scouting days. He shook it gently to check the fuel level and was rewarded by a nearly full sloshing sound. Now if only he had a match. He turned the lantern idly in his hands. It was useless without a match. He stopped turning the lantern and broke into a wide grin. Half a dozen wooden stove matches were secured to one portion of the glass with a piece of black electrical tape. Brent whistled softly to himself. Somebody around here was a paragon of efficiency. Someone who used this cave often. The lantern was a clear invitation to continue onward.

Brent set the lantern on the ground. Removing one of the matches, he ignited it by scraping it on the floor. After it had flared up and then settled down to a steady flame, he applied it to the wick and adjusted the trim. Along with a burst of light, the lantern emitted a familiar hiss with nostalgic associations. And the slight, pulsating heat thrown off by the lamp felt good too. He now felt ready to explore the unknown tunnel that lay ahead. If Melissa had preceded him, alone or with the unknown provisioner, that was where he belonged. If not, he would know soon enough.

This time he crawled into the tunnel on hands and knees with more confidence than he had felt before. Supporting himself with the palm of his left hand, he held the lantern by its support ring in his right hand. For the first twenty feet or so, the tunnel was level and straight, but then it engaged in a series of twists and turns, and the ground slope varied widely from true horizontal. Thanks to the lantern, however, Brent could see what lay ahead and thus anticipate his moves.

Now he could see that the height of the tunnel was about to diminish. Straight ahead, the slate-gray ceiling suddenly began to angle down toward the floor in a sharp V shape. It reminded him of an old Flemish painting in which the artist had used a similar exaggerated V shape to create the illusion of distance.

He sank back on his haunches and rested the lantern on the ground. He wasn't particularly claustrophobic, but it looked like a tight squeeze ahead. He prayed that this tunnel didn't simply peter out in a constricted dead end. If it did, then he had just wasted the last ten minutes. He grasped the handle of the lantern and began crawling forward with more urgency.

He soon found that crawling on all fours was going to be impossible. He was going to have to crawl on his stomach past the next bend in the tunnel to discover whether it went on or simply came to a dead end. Well, he had come this far; he might as well see it through to the end.

He established a workable rhythm. First, he slid the lantern forward on the ground as far as his fingers could stretch. Then he crawled right up next to it, reached over with his right hand, and shoved it forward again. The process was slow and the ground was uncomfortably hard, but it resulted in steady, forward progress.

Finally, he reached the bend in the tunnel. He shoved the lantern around the turn and crawled after it. He could see that the tunnel went on. But now, disconcertingly, it also became narrower. If he was to continue onward, he would have to keep the lantern in front of him at all times. There was no longer room enough to crawl up next to it. The effect would be a shorter and slower cycle of movement. Another effect also occurred to him: Up ahead, he would no longer be able to turn around. If he decided to return to the antechamber during the upcoming stretch, he would have no choice but to crawl blindly backward.

He considered the situation for a moment. The absolute silence that pressed in on him had an almost menacing quality to it. Now that he thought about it, the isolation he was experiencing here underground felt oppressively total. In some inexplicable way, it was so powerful that it seemed to be almost palpable. Instead of feeling like the lack of companionship, like an absence, it was like a presence. He had never felt anything quite like this before. Even though he had experienced his fair share of being alone, he had never felt so completely immersed in aloneness. It was as if he had kicked free of the rest of the universe.

It wasn't just fear that was toying with him, though he had to admit that facing the unknown around every bend in the tunnel was not his idea of comfort. No, it was the unfamiliarity, the strangeness of his own sensory responses. His eyes missed the sweep and the variety to which they were accustomed. Here, they saw only the close and unrelieved rock surfaces. His ears missed their usual expanded range of high and low pitches. In this tunnel, there was no variety of sound through which his ears could sort and choose. There were only the sounds of his breathing and crawling, the hiss of the lantern, and the scraping of its base on raw rock, and those had a strange, dampened quality, as if they were sounds merely remembered, not sounds being experienced. And the very smell of the air was alien. Because of the inexplicable breeze, it was not exactly stuffy, but it reminded him vaguely of the essence of exotic mushrooms.

Brent raised his eyebrows as all the data suddenly came together in instant recognition. This was the sort of thing that Edgar Allan Poe had so morbidly written about. This place reminded him of a tomb, an inescapable sepulcher. There was a finality about it that was overwhelming.

But he resolved *not* to be overwhelmed. He was here by choice. He was not trapped. He was certainly not buried alive. He would go on.

He pushed the lantern forward and followed it by paddling with his elbows and knees. His movements acquired a sort of swimming motion, a motion entirely appropriate in an atmosphere akin to being immersed in a thick, viscous liquid.

He had crawled about fifty feet when something impinged on his consciousness. He paused in the act of pushing the lantern forward, his fingertips barely grazing its metal base. Water. Dripping water. That was the sound he was now aware of. And there was also something different about the quality of the reflected light in the tunnel ahead. It no longer looked like a long, uninterrupted cylinder. Instead, about ten feet away, the tunnel seemed to break off and be swallowed by darkness. It simply disappeared.

He crawled forward cautiously, reducing each forward sliding motion to just inches at a time. As he drew within a few feet of the dark area, he grew certain of what he had merely suspected before. The tunnel was indeed running out, but it did not simply come to a dead end. Instead, it opened into a massive cavern.

Chapter Seven

Brent stopped a few inches from the end of the tunnel and grasped the handle of the lantern firmly in his left hand. The last thing that he needed was to push the lantern over the edge and lose his only source of light. Cautiously, he crept forward until his head and shoulders had cleared the rim of the tunnel.

Two feet below him, there was a ledge. If he slid forward a little more, he could deposit the lantern on the ledge and then ease himself after it, hands first. It would be a bit awkward as he pulled the rest of his body out of the tunnel entrance, but there was no way to turn around and come out feet first.

He reached down, supported his weight on his right hand, and deposited the lantern on the rock. The instant that he let go of the supporting ring, his hand froze in midair as the shock of the unexpected immobilized him. The light from the lantern had revealed a pair of combat boots.

Before he could either slide forward or scoot backward, Brent was seized roughly by the shoulders and pulled to the ground. When he rolled over on his back, wincing from the shooting pain in his ribs, he found himself looking up the barrel of an automatic weapon.

A voice barked out a command. Brent could not translate the words, but it soon became apparent what they had meant. From various parts of the cavern, matches were struck and a dozen lanterns and torches flared up. They came nowhere near adequately illuminating the soaring cavern, but they did begin to give Brent an idea of its dimensions. Noting the sources of light also gave him a quick, minimum body count.

The cavern seemed to be every bit as large as some of the European cathedrals that he had visited in his travels. In fact, with its oblong shape and natural vaulted ceiling, it even looked very much like a cathedral. The resemblance ended there, however. In place of pews, the floor in Brent's immediate vicinity held neat stacks of weapons, mostly bolt-action rifles and boxes of supplies. Everything in sight looked out of date but serviceable.

Someone sidled up to Brent and nudged him in the arm with the toe of a boot to get his attention. "The Yankee spy, is it not? We did not expect to capture *you* in our net, but we gladly accept whatever game fate sends our way."

The voice was a surprise. The urbane British accent and the careful articulation gave an impression of culture and sophistication. Educated at Sandhurst, no doubt. The officer, however, had a dumpy build and coarse features. Brent pondered the incongruity as he raised himself to a sitting position. He would have expected a voice more like Hulk Hogan's to come from such a bulky figure.

The officer added, "We have been hoping to snare

your rebel friends in their lair, but they seem to be in short supply of late. No matter. They will someday have need of this equipment, and then they will have to deal with us.''

Brent's eyes swept over the weapons again. Of course. That explained the vintage equipment stored in this cavern. The government forces were supplied with more modern weapons than the rebels—that is, until the U.S. shipments to Taamrat and his forces began to arrive in the near future. These hostiles had stumbled upon a rebel cache, and Brent had been unlucky enough to stumble upon *them*. Brent also noted, with enormous relief, that the officer had not so much as mentioned Melissa. She didn't appear to be in their clutches, and that was good news.

''I suppose you wouldn't be willing to tell us where the owners of these antique weapons are hiding.'' The officer waved a hand contemptuously toward the stacks of rifles. He looked down and read Brent's tight smile. ''No, I didn't think so. Well, perhaps a little time to reconsider will be salutary.'' He rocked slightly on the balls of his feet. ''Long before your rebel friends found this underground maze, we claimed it as our own for various . . . projects, shall we say? We have a little reception room where you can cool your heels for a while.''

He turned and issued an order. Two men swept forward and seized Brent firmly by the wrists. Before he could rise to his feet, they dragged him backward, his back and rump sliding along the rocky surface. The officer followed with a jaunty gait, a swagger stick tucked under his right arm. He was accompanied by an aide holding a lantern in each hand. After a few hundred yards, the detachment entered a corridor that led away from the main cavern. They continued for another few dozen yards, still dragging Brent ignominiously along the ground. Suddenly, without warning, they dumped him in front of a plank door. He noted that it was secured from the outside by a stout wooden bar inserted in two iron brackets.

"My accommodations, no doubt." Brent directed his comment to the officer who once again stood over him, arms akimbo.

"Quite right. You will be a guest of the state while you think things over." The man slapped his left palm with the end of the swagger stick. "I will not be so boorish as to issue dire and useless threats. I think you can tell that we mean business. Or you shortly will." His eyes bored relentlessly into Brent's. Brent stared right back unblinkingly, but part of him had to admit that the man's understatement was impressive.

The officer stepped around Brent, grasped the swagger stick firmly in his right hand, and began to pound loudly and vigorously on the door. Even as the officer drummed away on the planks, two of the soldiers reached down, grasped Brent under the arms, and raised him to a standing position in one smooth motion. They forced him toward the door as the officer lifted the wooden bar in both hands and pushed the creaking door slightly inward with his boot. As Brent was shoved into the dark interior, he was startled to find a kerosene lantern thrust into his hands by the aide. As he stumbled forward, the door slammed behind him and the bar thudded firmly into place. Receding footsteps told him that he was now alone.

The circle of light from the flickering lantern cast distorted shadows on the dim walls, giving them the illusion of a wavy motion. But it was the insistent smell that assaulted Brent like a pounding fist and demanded his immediate attention. Compounded of mustiness and decay, it clogged his airways and induced gagging. He raised his free hand in a useless attempt to shield his nostrils.

And then there was that vague rustling, a slithery sound, a stealthy, subterranean whisper that barely reached the threshold of hearing but that caused the hairs on the back of his neck to rise in instant wariness. Most disconcerting of all was the constant illusion of motion beyond the fringe of light, the perception of undulating walls and floor, the feeling that solid materials were rippling and writhing in a nervous series of waves.

Brent raised the lantern higher and took a cautious step forward. Impossibly, the floor seemed to part and recede as he stepped forward. It was as if a carpet were being rolled back as he approached. At the same time, the background sound level rose. The barely perceptible rustle became a whir of activity, a sound of slipping and sliding and scrambling to get away.

And then, clearly defined within the circle of light, a large rat, bolder than the rest, streaked across the floor within inches of Brent's bare feet. Involuntarily, Brent clenched his teeth and parted his lips in a primitive grimace of disgust. At the same time, he jumped back, only to feel something soft and protesting under his heel. He whirled around, lantern extended, in time to see a blur of dark, furry bodies scramble to escape the painful glare of the light.

And now, tribally disturbed, the rats began to chatter and squeal in protest of this invasion of their privacy, and the walls and floor became a roller coaster of activity as furry bodies slid over and against one another as they raced around insanely. As if alive, the walls and outer reaches of the floor alternately swelled and receded like a huge living membrane.

Stunned, Brent continued to turn in a slow circle, lantern held at arm's length, in an attempt to preserve his small circle of safety. But he knew that the light would eventually stop being a threat to these creatures and that they would begin to close the circle and creep closer and closer to this intruder.

As he rotated in a clockwise direction, he began to notice that the walls, at regularly spaced intervals, projected outward slightly. Since these bulges, along with everything else, were covered by thousands of writhing rats, he could not tell exactly what they were, but what if they turned out to be the outlines of other doorways, or the blocked entrances to radiating tunnels? What if they offered a means of escape?

He stopped and picked out a bulge that seemed more prominent than the rest. Slowly, he began to step forward, closing the gap between himself and the rat-covered shape. Furry bodies tumbled and squealed as they scrambled to get out of his way, and the surface of the wall began to be discernible in that one narrow area. Brent froze in his tracks and blanched.

As the gray carcasses oozed away from the shaft of light, they left uncovered a skeleton chained to the wall. A few of the bolder rats scurried over and through the rib cage, causing the skeleton to sway slightly on rusty, creaking chains. Brent watched in horror as a lean rat leaped nimbly up to the grinning skull, scampered through one empty eye socket, and emerged through the other, and finally came to rest on the very top of the skull, where it began to groom a long, hairless tail.

Brent backed away from the wall, and soon the skeleton had disappeared from view once again as a living shroud of rats covered it completely. Brent whirled and faced the plank door. The only way out, it appeared, was the way that he had entered. But the door was solidly barred from the outside, and he had no tools. Slowly, he approached the door, trying not to step on any of the forms that scampered across the floor only inches in front of his toes.

He ran his hand over the rough wooden surface, careful not to snag a splinter. The only irregularities were the protruding slotted bolt heads that apparently held the metal brackets on the other side of the door in place. *If only I had a screwdriver,* he thought. He looked at the lantern in his hand and began to rotate it speculatively. His eye was caught by the metal screw-on cap that sealed the kerosene chamber. He squatted and set the lantern on the floor. Using the fingers of his right hand, he overcame the initial tightness and resistance and began to unscrew the cap. With a final twist, he held it in his hand.

Leaving the lantern on the ground right in front of the door, he set to work trying to loosen the bolts with the inner edge of the cap. But the bolts had been in place for decades if not centuries, and they would not budge a single millimeter. All that he succeeded in doing was to twist the cap impossibly out of shape. It would never go back on the lantern again.

He threw it disgustedly to the floor, and when it stopped bouncing, it was surrounded by a horde of curious rats who sniffed at it and reached out to touch it with nervous, clawed feet. He shifted away from them until his back rested against the door and he could go no farther. He sank to the ground, moved the lantern between his feet, and watched the restless sea of rats in its unceasing motion.

The penetrating smell of kerosene competed momentarily with the dank smell of the chamber. Brent looked down at the lantern, and an idea began to form. He picked the lantern up by its base and shook it gently. The sloshing sound told him that although it was not full, it did have quite a bit of fuel remaining. He swiveled around and studied the surface of the door. The wood planks looked old and dry. Good news for a change.

Brent rose to his feet, and careful not to let the kerosene splash against the hot glass panels over the flame, he began to slosh and drip kerosene over the surface of the door, especially in the area of the bolts. If a controlled fire could weaken that area, he might be able to work the brackets loose somehow.

The light began to flicker ominously, so he quickly turned the lantern back upright and held it steady for a moment. The height of the flame increased, but it was not nearly as steady and strong as it had been. And it may just have been his imagination, but Brent could swear that the circle of rats was moving closer to him as the light grew dimmer. Before he lost the flame entirely, he had to ignite that door.

He dripped a small pool of kerosene on the ground under the door and then backed away from it. He eyed the distance carefully, held his left hand ready to shield his face, then hurled the lamp at the base of the door. It smashed against the stone surface with a clatter of metal and the tinkling of shattering glass. A loud whoosh and a blinding glare signaled instant success. Tongues of flame raced up the surface of the plank door, and soon the old, dry wood was crackling and blazing.

And then the horde of rats went insane in panic. Squealing with deafening intensity, they began to race around the room away from the door in a tight circle. Like a runaway merry-go-round, they twirled and spun at top speed. Brent planted his feet firmly and raised both arms to shield his head and face. Oblivious now to his presence, the rats swarmed around and over him, nearly knocking him off balance from time to time by the collective weight of their flying wedge against his ankles. Many of them climbed up and over him as if he were a pillar standing in the way.

As the chamber filled with smoke, Brent's eyes began to water and he started to cough. He knew that he would have to make a move toward the door very soon, before the oxygen in the room was gone. But he did not relish trying to walk on the flying carpet of furry bodies that reeled all around him. Perhaps he should use a sliding motion instead of lifting and planting his feet.

But before he could take a step, he heard the approach of shouting voices in the corridor outside. The blaze had been noticed. Soon he heard the sound of the wooden bar hitting the floor as someone knocked it out of its brackets. This was followed by the thud of boots on the door, which swung back to reveal three armed guards with fury on their faces and automatic rifles in their hands.

But their fury turned to horror when the rats, suddenly sensing an escape route, turned en masse and began to streak out the door into the corridor. As if one with their intent, Brent surged forward and joined the headlong rush. Two of the startled guards fell to the floor as a wall of rats surged against them. Their screams rent the air as they all but disappeared, arms and legs flailing, under a swarm of furry bodies. The third guard stood his ground desperately, swinging his rifle like a club in a futile attempt to stem the invasion. Brent smashed a fist into the guard's jaw, deftly catching his rifle in midair as the man released it and fell to the floor unconscious.

Brent stood there for a moment, the rifle pointed in readiness, and weighed his chances. To go back to the main cavern was to face perhaps a dozen remaining government troops. And with the smoke drifting down the corridor toward the main cavern where the troops were temporarily billeted, there could be no element of surprise. But the smoke drifting down the corridor in their direction was revealing. It meant that prevailing air currents were pouring in from the other direction. And where there was air, there was a source for the air, a breach to the outside. Brent turned and ran in that direction.

When he reached the end of the area lit by the blazing door, he slowed down. From this point on, without a lantern, it was going to be strictly feel as you go. He would have to work his way through absolute darkness in an underground area that was totally unfamiliar. He wondered if he would be better off chancing the twelve-to-one odds that lay in the opposite direction. Only time would tell.

And now began hours of painfully slow progress as he wandered blindly through endless miles of tunnels. Some of them turned out to be cul-de-sacs, and each time he reached a dead end, he had to retrace his steps wearily until he reached an earlier branch leading off in another direction. He began to use the rifle much as an unsighted person would use a cane, probing the floor slightly ahead before planting his feet. His other hand trailed along the wall at waist height so that branching corridors would not be missed in the inky darkness. From time to time he slumped to the ground to rest, but a sense of urgency soon caused him to move on.

Now, as he inched his way down yet another narrow passageway, he noticed that the footing was becoming treacherous. For one thing, the floor here was damp. In fact, his feet occasionally slid through little pools of what he fervently hoped was water. For another thing, there now seemed to be a definite tilt to the surface upon which he was walking. In fact, he was beginning to slide a bit uncontrollably on the increasingly slippery rock.

Suddenly, his feet shot out from under him and he landed painfully on his tailbone. Before he had time to try to stand up, he found himself slipping inexorably forward. Even without light to illuminate the area, it was obvious that the downward slope had increased sharply. He tried using the butt of the rifle to stop his forward motion, but it simply slid along the smooth ground with him. He reached out with his free hand to grasp the wall, but all it encountered was a damp, slimy surface that allowed no fingerhold whatsoever.

As the ground surface fell away before him like a playground slide, his momentum increased. He could feel a slight breeze on his face, and he experienced a growing sense of queasiness as his body followed the contours of the passageway that bounced him from side to side as he hurtled downward in total darkness. More desperate now, he reached out frantically with his right hand to find an outcrop or a hole, anything at all to grab on to. He raised his hand over his head and was startled to find that the roof of the tunnel was now within reach. If he had been standing, there wouldn't be enough headroom to walk upright.

And then his hand encountered a rock formation that hung from the ceiling like a stalactite. Instinctively, he dropped the rifle, and his other hand shot up to secure his hold. For the next few seconds, he could hear a grating sound as the rifle continued to slide downward. Then, suddenly and inexplicably, there was an eerie silence. It was as if the rifle had been snatched from the face of the earth. A while later he heard a faint splash.

His stomach lurched as he recognized what those sounds meant and the fate that he had, temporarily at least, narrowly avoided. For if he had continued to slide, he would have reached the end of the chute, been catapulted into midair, and then fallen helplessly at thirty-two feet per second until his body plunged into the water far below. And that was assuming that he would have been lucky enough to land in deep water instead of on a rock formation.

Brent gripped the stalactite even more firmly, resisting the pull of gravity. He could not hold on indefinitely. He knew that his fingers would eventually lose their grip, or that his straining arm muscles would begin to tremble with fatigue before giving out. In the next couple of minutes, a dozen unsuccessful attempts to pull himself to his feet in order to turn around and head back up the passageway convinced him that it was too steep and too slippery.

The best that he could do was to pull his knees up to his chest. Having gotten that far, he extended his legs at right angles to his trunk until his feet touched the wall. Pushing against that wall with the soles of his feet, he slid backward until his shoulders bunched up against the opposite wall. In this way, he managed to wedge his body sideways in the chute, all the while clinging fiercely to the stalactite that had halted his slide to destruction. Now, at least, he had a three-point stance and could take some of his weight off his hands and arms, although he dared not let go entirely. But all that he had really done, he realized, was to buy a short reprieve. The thought of a reprieve made him think suddenly and achingly of Melissa. Did she, too, have the luxury of a reprieve? Was she, even at this very moment, clinging to life somewhere?

How long he lay wedged there he did not know, but it seemed forever. And then his senses began to play tricks on him. He thought he heard a murmur of voices and detected the slightest scintillations of light, like the distant stirrings of a long-awaited dawn. He closed his eyes in despair and weariness. He knew that sensory deprivation produces hallucinations, but no one wants to admit it when it occurs. It seems weak, somehow. He opened his eyes again. No! This was no hallucination. There actually *was* some light. He could see the faintest outlines of the rock around him, particularly a gleam from wet surfaces.

He turned his head. Up the tunnel, in the direction from which he had come, there was the sound of activity and an increasing glow of light. His heart sank as he realized that the government troops had caught up with him. Talk about mixed feelings. He was about to be freed from one dilemma only to be plunged into another. But where there was life, there was hope. He decided to make his presence known. He needed help and couldn't afford to be choosy about its source. "Hello!" he yelled. "Down here! Help!"

A babble of voices rose excitedly. Everything depended now on whether he was still of use to his enemies. If not, they could always slide something heavy like a boulder down the chute to dislodge him. He waited. More light was aimed in his direction, and after a few minutes he heard something sliding toward him. Anxiously, he listened to determine what it was. It sounded like a controlled slide; it didn't have the insistent rhythm of something accelerating or careening out of control. He grunted in relief.

Before long, a head appeared, then a set of wide shoulders, and then the rest of a muscular black man who was dressed in fatigues and secured with a stout rope around his waist. When he came within reach of Brent, he turned and shouted something over his shoulder. His forward progress stopped immediately. Evidently, unlike the officer whom Brent had encountered earlier, this soldier didn't speak English. He motioned to Brent to grab on to the rope, and when Brent's grip was secure, the soldier seized Brent's belt with both hands and shouted back over his shoulder again. The rope grew taut, and then Brent and his rescuer were pulled back up the slippery incline. As he slid along, Brent prepared himself for the retaliations that would surely come. This time, he did not expect understatement and subtlety to be the order of the day. When they reached level ground and came within a foot or so of the two men who were pulling on the rope, Brent tensed as he waited for the blow on the head that was sure to follow.

"Mr. Collins! This is unexpected, to be sure. I had no thought that the falling rifle was from you." The voice, lilting in its accent, came from a robed figure in the background. "Help him, help him," he went on. "He is a friend." Instantly, Brent felt supporting arms grasp him from either side, pull him upright, and deposit him gently on the ground.

His spirits soared with relief as he recognized the voice of the goatherd who had rescued him from the quicksand. Once again, they were meeting on opposite ends of a rope. "Unless I am mistaken, this has to be Mr. Fankara," Brent said. He reached out a hand and found it gripped in an enthusiastic handshake.

"Please call me Yakob. Mr. Fankara makes me feel old, don't you know." He chuckled infectiously. "But I forget my hospitalities. Let us get you some dry clothes. Come, come."

Later, in a nearby small cavern, Brent changed into borrowed fatigues and gratefully accepted some water. He took a lingering swig from the canteen and then turned his undivided attention to Yakob. "So you're part of Taamrat's rebel forces, then. I was wondering where you fit into the picture when we met for the first time."

"To be sure. I am commanding in this region. We are . . . how do you say . . . plotting? Yes, plotting to get back the guns that our enemies have stolen from us." As Yakob gestured over his left shoulder, Brent assumed that that was the direction of the larger cavern where he had encountered the government troops and the rats. A look of concern crossed Yakob's face. ''But tell me, please, how do you come upon this underground place? I must know. We did not think to be so easy to find. First the government soldiers, you see. Then you.'' He extended his hands in exasperation.

Brent hastened to reassure him that it had been entirely accidental. Then he went on to explain in detail how he and Melissa had been forced to plunge into the river to avoid capture or death at the hands of loyalist troops. He ended his account with a question to which he feared he already knew the answer: ''Have you or any of your men seen her? Do you have any idea where she might be?''

Yakob turned to his men and addressed them in another language. Their negative headshaking confirmed Brent's gloomy fears. At best, Melissa must have been swept downstream. At worst. . . . But he refused to consider the worst.

After listening intently to Yakob, two men broke away from the group and took off toward the far end of the cavern. Yakob turned back to Brent and said, ''They shall see what is to see. In the meanwhile, eat something with me.'' He looked down at Brent's scraped and bruised bare feet. ''And perhaps let me give to you some boots. I do not think you enjoy the hard stones, no?''

An hour later, a clearer picture of Melissa's fate emerged when the two soldiers returned and huddled with Yakob. After much listening and nodding, he translated their report to Brent. A nomadic shepherd had told them of seeing a white woman with yellow hair. She had waded ashore downstream that very morning, near a small village called Bitwad.

"But I know this place!" Yakob exclaimed. "I have in that village many cousins." He hesitated.

Brent read his hesitation. "But there's a problem, right?"

"It *is* a problem there, my friend. Although the people of Bitwad are liking our cause, there is also in that village a station of enemy soldiers."

"How many soldiers?"

"Perhaps five and twenty. Perhaps less few."

"Heavily armed?"

"Heavily enough. Many automatics."

Brent sensed that there was even more to come and that it would not be good news. He faced it squarely and forced the issue: "And is there anything else that I should know?"

"Alas, since you ask, I fear so. They say that in this station of soldiers, there is visiting today one who is a special enemy of my people. This man has caused many orphans and widows. This man we call Yämärgän."

Brent felt his blood run cold. Of all the people into whose hands Melissa could have fallen, this had to be the worst.

"Ah, I see from your face that you know of this name. I am sorry this has to be, and sorry I am the one to tell of it, but. . . ." Yakob turned his palms upward in a gesture of helplessness.

"It's not your fault, of course. But thank you." Brent cleared his throat. "Look, is there some way that I can get to this village—quickly?"

Yakob nodded emphatically. "Yes. Even now I am making preparations. We will leave this moment, you and I." He rose and threw a fold of his robe over his shoulder.

"Yakob, I really appreciate that, but this is my problem. I don't want you getting involved unnecessarily. You've got a revolution to take care of."

Yakob looked at him with forbearance on his face. "On the radio," he said, "Taamrat said to me that you are a man very brave, very daring. He spoke truly. But do you know this village of Bitwad? No. And do you know the way to get there? No. But Yakob does. So this moment we will leave, you *and* I."

Brent found it hard to argue with the man's logic. He also sensed that Yakob was intractable once his mind was made up. So he fell into step behind Yakob and followed him to the exit.

Chapter Eight

Half an hour later, Brent found himself drifting along at an altitude of two hundred feet in the backseat of a rickety Curtiss biplane. Yakob was piloting the craft, as much as it could be said to respond to the controls. When Brent first laid eyes on the biplane after emerging from the cavern, his jaw fell and he found himself speechless. He had never seen one outside the walls of the National Air Museum, let alone flown in one. Yakob informed him proudly of its pedigree. Over the years it had been used for crop dusting, postal deliveries, and private passenger service, and it may even have seen action in World War I, or so the previous owner had claimed.

Once airborne, the engine had an alarming tendency to sputter, and the open cockpit was incredibly noisy and windblown, but the plane did cut across impossible terrain in the straightest possible line. It was a white-knuckle special, but it certainly beat driving hundreds of miles out of the way to get around canyons and mountains and other natural obstacles. Time was of the essence.

They had been following the meanderings of the Awash

River, and now Yakob turned in his seat and shouted over the noise of the engine: "Behind these coming mountains, Bitwad." Brent signaled his understanding. Yakob turned back and pointed slightly to the right to pinpoint the exact peak. He began to bank the plane in a very leisurely right turn. Brent was not surprised. He had learned by now that the plane did nothing quickly.

It soon became apparent that they would need more altitude to clear the peak dead ahead. Yakob, of course, had anticipated that, and the set of his shoulders indicated that he was already pulling back steadily on the stick. Still, as the plane drifted closer to the mountain, Brent had the uncomfortable feeling that it was not rising as quickly as it should.

He saw Yakob jerk sharply at the stick a few times and shake his head. The peak came closer and closer, filling the horizon over Yakob's head and shoulders. Now Yakob was half-rising from his seat with the effort of pulling back on the stick. Brent watched in horror as the peak loomed right in front of them. They had gained some altitude, but they were still going to slam into the very top of the peak. They were not going to clear it.

Brent closed his eyes at the last second. He did not want to see this. Suddenly, he felt a heavy bump and his head was thrown back against the padded seat. As the engine sputtered on, he opened his eyes and turned around quickly. The peak was receding just behind the tail of the plane. He could see two puffs of dust where the landing gear had scraped across the grimy surface of the rock.

Grinning, Yakob turned around and held up two fingers

forming a V. *Some victory,* Brent thought, finally releasing his breath. It felt more like a reprieve.

Yakob was soon pointing excitedly to some branch-roofed buildings hugging the contours of a valley and wedged between outcroppings of lava rock. There were perhaps two dozen buildings in all, many of them with attached corrals, and the village was dominated by a church with a gleaming steeple. Perched next to it was a long, flat building with a shiny metal roof, the only one of its type in the village. A large, wavy red cross was painted on the corrugated roof.

Yakob turned to shout an explanation: "The clinic. It is of importance in this region. The only one, you see." He turned back to his task in time to see soldiers running out of the clinic and into the dusty road where they stood pointing up at the plane. Yakob banked to the left and went for more altitude. Brent saw the point of the maneuver immediately. It wouldn't be long before the soldiers started firing at the low-flying intruder. Humble though it was, it was part of the rebel air force.

And almost before he had completed the thought, several soldiers below did begin to open fire. Brent ducked down involuntarily into his seat as he heard the reports, but straightened up the instant he caught himself doing it. It was folly, of course. Nothing could stop bullets from coming through the thin covering beneath his feet. He and Yakob were at the mercy of the marksmanship of the troops below.

Yakob continued the banking maneuver until the shadow of the plane had completed a circle around the edge of the village. Then he straightened out and flew southwest in the direction of some precipitous ridges. In vain, Brent scoured the landscape for a large field or level surface that could serve as a landing field.

Yakob caught his attention, and then reached back, attempting to hand him something. Brent stretched forward until he could grasp the object, a holster and belt. He opened the flap. Nestled within was a Webley with a pearl handle. Brent smiled. It was vintage, but the unmistakable smell of gun oil told him that it had been well taken care of. He had no doubt that it would be reliable.

As Yakob signaled again, Brent leaned forward to hear. "I will go down to skip the surface, no? You will jump when I signal, okay?"

Brent sat there stunned for a moment. They weren't going to land. And Yakob was evidently asking him to bail out without a parachute. Was the man crazy? Then it occurred to Brent that it would, in fact, be perfectly possible because of the nature of their plane. One of the characteristics of a biplane is that it can fly at a very low speed just short of stalling out. If Yakob took it low enough, Brent supposed that it would be no worse than jumping out of a car doing about thirty or forty miles an hour, and that was something that he had been trained to do. It was simply a matter of tuck and roll.

He looked at Yakob, who was sitting there expectantly. Then he nodded his head and said, "Okay, Yakob, let's do it." He began to strap the holster around his waist.

Yakob gave him a thumbs-up sign. "Very good. 'Geronimo!' as you Americans say."

By now, they had drifted over the ridge system about a mile southwest of the village. Yakob banked the plane and began to fly parallel to the ridge. He leaned out of his cockpit, scanning the terrain below. A little later he pointed to a small grassy plateau straight ahead. It looked better to Brent than anything else in sight, and he leaned forward, tapped Yakob on the shoulder, and said, "That's a good one."

Yakob nodded vigorously and began to bring the plane around for a low-level pass. As they drew nearer to the ground, Brent could hear the engine losing some of its vigor as Yakob trimmed the throttle. It was time to move, and Brent hoisted himself up on his seat until he was standing on it. Then, grasping the edge of the cockpit with both hands, he stepped out backward onto the trailing surface of the left wing. Even at this reduced speed, the wind tore at him, trying to pull him from his precarious perch. He tucked in his chin and reached out with his left hand for a strut. His fingers closed tightly around it. Then he released his hold on the edge of the cockpit and lunged for the same strut with his right hand, fighting fierce wind resistance all the way. Little by little, he began to inch his way along the wing, hand over hand, strut by strut, feet sliding carefully, until he was halfway across the back portion of the wing.

For his part, Yakob flew as steadily as anyone could, compensating for the extra weight on the wing, reducing speed to just short of a stall, and zooming down with pinpoint accuracy over the chosen target on the first attempt. Soon they were skimming over the ridge so low that it seemed they would be landing. Engine thrust had been reduced so much that the plane seemed to be shuddering on the verge of a stall. Faster than Brent would have liked, the flat, clear surface rushed toward him.

He heard Yakob yell something but could not make

out the actual words. Then he released his fierce grip on the strut and stepped backward off the wing into nothingness. He dropped about four feet, landing on his heels with a wrenching jolt. Instantly, he pulled his knees toward his chest, hunched his shoulders in the same direction, and crossed his arms one over the other in front of his chest.

As momentum threw him inexorably forward, he turned slightly in midair before slamming into the ground so that he would land on his side. Leg, hip, side, and shoulder hit the ground in quick sequence. Tucking his head in as tightly as he could, he felt the back of his neck hit last as he began to tumble forward.

He did not try to slow his motion in any way, because it would have been futile and a sure way to get seriously hurt. Instead, he rolled end over end eight or nine times, allowing momentum to take its natural course. By the last couple of revolutions of his body, he had come out of the tuck and was rolling sideways fully extended, arms held rigidly against his side. He ended up tipping over onto his hands and knees.

Yakob was circling back at a higher altitude to check on him. Brent stood and waved with both arms as the plane zoomed over and turned back toward the village. He assumed that Yakob would do one last flyby over the clinic to convince the soldiers that he was returning to base and to keep their attention away from Brent. Given the terrain, they should not have seen his bailout.

He leaned down and brushed off his pants as best he could. The grass stains remained. The leather jacket that Yakob had found for him was scuffed, but it had saved his own hide from being scratched and scraped. He looked in the direction of the village. It was out of sight, but he could hear a volley of distant shots, no doubt aimed at the diminishing drone of the biplane. It was time to move.

Brent kept to rifts and gullies rather than the more exposed heights of ridges and plateaus. It was uphill work, because the village was at the foot of the volcanic mountain, but vigorous exercise had always been part of his daily routine. For an agent in the field, it was as necessary as eating.

Finally, the outskirts of the village came into view, and Brent could see six laughing and squealing children playing next to a corral with two goats. With civilians in the area, this was going to be very tricky. He crouched down and moved through a gully away from the children toward the center of the village. He wanted to come up behind the clinic. That was where the soldiers had emerged when he and Yakob first flew over. It was the only official-looking building in town. He had no doubt that the soldiers had taken it over as their headquarters.

He raised his head until he was able to look over the lip of the gully. There was the back of the church, its whitewashed walls gleaming under the onslaught of the late-afternoon sun, and next to it was the back of the clinic. Three women dressed in identical reddish-brown *shamas* stood in the dusty plaza in front of the church and the clinic. They talked animatedly, their large, plaited baskets balanced gracefully on their heads. He guessed that the topic of conversation was the biplane that had just brought some excitement into village life.

After a few minutes the group broke up and moved in different directions. This was his chance, and he pulled himself up and climbed out of the gully. Without hesitating, he crawled swiftly to the back of the clinic. From the open window a few feet above his head, he could hear raucous laughter and loud voices. The troops were probably congratulating themselves after fighting off a full-scale rebel air attack. Of such slender incidents were barracks stories born. He had told a few himself.

Suddenly, he heard footsteps coming from around the corner. Someone was walking toward the back of the clinic. The heavy steps were unhurried, so Brent probably had not been spotted, but they sounded like the steps of an adult man in boots. Assuming that it was a soldier on patrol, he crept toward the left corner of the building, hugging the wall.

Quietly, he pulled back the holster flap with his right hand and extracted the Webley. He turned it in his hand, grasping it by the barrel. He could not afford to fire it and draw attention to himself, so he would have to use it as a bludgeon. He flattened himself against the building and timed his movements carefully.

The crunching boots were about to turn the corner. Brent stood on tiptoe and raised the weapon high above his head. The instant the soldier appeared around the corner, Brent slammed the butt against the man's temple. With a whooshing intake of breath, the soldier crumpled into his arms.

Brent dragged him backward until his feet no longer extended beyond the corner of the building. Then he dropped him and checked the soldier's pulse. He was alive but would be out of action for quite some time. Brent shoved the gun back into its holster.

He rose carefully to his feet and eased upward to the sill of the open window. He could still hear a steady murmur of voices, but they seemed to be emanating from a more distant room. He raised his head quickly to look inside the room and just as quickly crouched back down.

It was a small medical examining room, complete with a traditional glass-door cabinet, a small sink, and a black vinyl examining table. What made it of overwhelming interest was that Melissa, bound and gagged, was strapped to the table. Her head was toward the window. She had not seen him.

He raised his head again, this time taking a longer look. Right now, no one else was in the room, and so he had better take advantage of this moment. He stood up and slid through the window headfirst, doing a silent somersault over the sill and coming to rest as quietly as possible on his feet. Lying just a few feet away, Melissa strained against her bonds to see what was going on behind her.

Brent moved swiftly to her side, his finger already on his lips. Though she could not speak because of the gag, he did not want any other reaction to betray his presence. When the initial shock of recognition had passed, her eyes filled with tears of joy and relief.

He reached for an edge of the gag and was about to push it away from her mouth when he heard footsteps in the hall outside. He patted her reassuringly on the shoulder, moved silently behind the examining table, and crouched behind its base right underneath her head. These footsteps were softer than the soldier's had been, almost dainty, in fact. But they were accompanied by a peculiar wheezing sound as if someone were exerting great effort simply to walk. Brent recognized the labored breathing.

He had no doubt that he was once again in the presence of Yämärgän.

As Yämärgän shuffled slowly into the room, his great bulk shut out much of the light streaming in from behind him. An ominous shadow preceded him like a warning, and it fell upon Melissa and darkened the hiding place where Brent crouched.

The door closed, bringing uniform shadows, and then the bright surgical ceiling lights leaped into action as Yämärgän clicked on the wall switch. He waddled forward and stopped at the foot of the table.

His low voice rumbled forth like muted thunder: "Have you thought, then, about our little talk? And are you ready to tell me things, my pigeon? Can we speak the truth to each other?" As he spoke, his voice modulated to a level that was soothing, almost hypnotic. He was practically crooning now, his voice an entreaty and a promise.

Brent heard him slide open a drawer at the other end of the examining table. Then he rooted about in what sounded like clinking silverware. This was followed by total silence except for the heavy sibilance of Yämärgän's breathing.

"Ah, *pobrecita*, I see fear in your eyes. But do not be afraid of these little instruments, my dove. These are only the friends of truth—*los amigos de verdad*. These little ones will merely coax you to share your secrets with me, to whisper in my ear what I must know. Here, let me show them to you. Let the light of their reflection fall upon your soft skin."

His voice was now a hoarse whisper. Brent felt absolute revulsion at its obscene, wheedling tone. If this monster so much as touched a hair of her head. . . .

Brent pulled back. Yämärgän was sidling around the table, and Brent had caught sight of his striped robe. He did not want to be seen until Yämärgän came within his reach. Now Brent could hear the creak of leather restraints and feel the vibrations of Melissa's agitated movements as she squirmed desperately to elude Yämärgän's grasp.

Brent could wait no longer, and rising up in one fluid movement, he rushed at Yämärgän's startled face with his fist cocked and ready to strike. As he drew within a foot of him, he shot his doubled fist forward with all his fury and exploded it straight into Yämärgän's piggish face. It connected with a satisfying splat, and immediately Yämärgän's nose began to bleed profusely. But the man did not shift one inch. He stood there, an uncomprehending look on his face, but showing no evidence of pain. Brent struck again, this time aiming for the solar plexus. His fist sank into a mound of yielding fat with no visible effect. It felt like hitting a punching bag filled with feathers instead of sand.

Yämärgän reached the end of his patience. He emitted a low growl and began to advance upon Brent. Simply by walking forward, he pushed Brent back inexorably. Though he crouched for leverage and resisted with all the strength in his arms, Brent could not stop Yämärgän's forward motion, and he suddenly realized that this man had the strength to crush him to death against the wall like a bug.

When Yämärgän reached the end of the examining table, he paused, but not because of Brent's efforts to stop him. Brent looked into his face and saw, to his utter horror, that Yämärgän was regarding Melissa's ivory neck with morbid interest. Yämärgän raised his hand high into the air and slowly, inexorably, began to bring it down. The glint of polished steel flashed from the surgical instrument as it descended relentlessly upon Melissa's unprotected throat.

Desperately, Brent grabbed Yämärgän's wrist in both hands in an effort to stay the downward progress of the scalpel. But he found himself being pushed down, a mere appendage to Yämärgän's arm, a useless barrier to his murderous intent.

In one last attempt to save Melissa, Brent released Yämärgän's wrist and dropped his hands to the table for leverage. Leaning to the left, he lashed up and out with his right foot, aiming straight for Yämärgän's impassive face with a lethal karate kick. It connected under his chin, snapping his head back and causing his fingers to release the scalpel. It dropped to the table, blade first, penetrating the vinyl cover and coming to rest next to Melissa's face.

Slowly, having lost his balance and about to lose consciousness, Yämärgän drifted backward, stumbling awkwardly in a futile attempt to keep his footing. Then his eyes rolled up in their sockets, his jaw dropped, and he began to fall like a felled tree. He landed heavily on his backside, shaking the room, and sank back against the closed door, his chin slumped down on his chest and his shoulders coming to rest against the groaning wood.

Brent stood there for a second, breathing heavily. Then he snatched up the scalpel and set about freeing Melissa. But as he cut through the leather straps binding her feet, someone knocked tentatively on the door.

"*Qué pasa, Jefe? Deseas ayuda?*"

Someone was asking if everything was all right, if

Yämärgän needed help. Evidently, noisy interrogations were his filthy trademark. Brent needed to buy time, and he cleared his throat and lowered his voice to a rumble. *"No deseo ayuda. Vaya!"* This order to go away was met with an awkward silence. Brent wasn't sure if he had been credible enough. He leaned over to Melissa and whispered desperately. "Quick, give a couple of screams!"

Without missing a beat, Melissa complied instantly. Perhaps her screams were born of desperation. Perhaps they represented residual terror from her ordeal. But they left absolutely no doubt that this was a woman in terminal trouble.

From the other side of the door, Brent could hear a loud, cruel laugh. Then came the words, *"Perdóname, Jefe,"* followed by receding footsteps. Whoever it was had believed them. They had been given the gift of time.

Brent completed the job of freeing Melissa, and then he scooped her up from the table and set her down on the floor. He looked into her face with concern, feeling an affection so deep that it startled him.

"Are you all right? I couldn't stand it when I looked in and saw you strapped to that table. I didn't know if you were alive or not. I couldn't have taken it if you'd been hurt."

"I'm all right. They didn't hurt me." A look of revulsion crossed her face as she caught sight of Yämärgän's body sprawled against the door. "But that man. The things he said and threatened. . . . Oh, Brent, until I saw your face, I thought it was all over."

Her eyes filled with tears and she leaned against his chest. He gathered her within the protective circle of his arms, vowing to himself never to allow her to fall into danger again.

Chapter Nine

O nce they had escaped through the clinic window, their top priority was to acquire a set of wheels. When Melissa had slipped safely into the gully to conceal herself until he returned with a liberated vehicle, Brent sprinted across to the back of the church. He crouched down in the shadow of a small porch for a few seconds to see if he had been noticed. When no alarm was raised, he cautiously ascended the three wooden steps and tried the doorknob.

He found himself in the sacristy. Straight ahead was an arched doorway that led out into the sanctuary where the altar was located. The sacristy wall to his left was entirely occupied by a set of vestment cases and an oak vesting table that looked like a long, low dresser with very wide drawers. The wall to his right held a sink, a floor-length mirror, a set of wooden pegs for hanging long garments, and a bulletin board to which was tacked an ecclesiastical calendar and several photographs of smiling altar boys.

Brent's eye was immediately attracted to a black hooded robe that hung from one of the pegs. If he hoped to move through the church and out into the street in search of a vehicle, this would certainly act as a disguise. Otherwise, he was certain to attract instant attention in his western clothing.

He took the monk's garment from the peg and slipped it on over his head. Beneath the robe, looped over the same peg, was a black leather belt about five feet long. Brent puzzled over its use for a moment until he caught sight of a priest in one of the pictures on the bulletin board. It showed that the belt went around the waist. One end slipped through a loop and then came back up and through to form a knot. He tried it, compared himself to the photo, and decided that he looked authentic enough. He pulled the hood over his head and walked solemnly through the door into the church.

Two elderly women knelt in separate pews, their heads bowed, and with rosary beads dangling from their fingers. They didn't even look up as he slipped quietly down a side aisle and headed toward the vestibule of the church. When he got to the large double doors, he opened the one on the right just enough to peer out into the street without being seen. Aside from a mangy dog scratching itself in the middle of the dusty road and an old man pushing a squeaking wheelbarrow, there was no sign of movement.

More interesting to Brent were the two military vehicles. The flatbed truck was parked at a careless angle in front of the clinic entrance. Its cab was empty and the door on the driver's side had been left open. Just in front of the church, enjoying the relative coolness provided by the long shadow that the steeple threw across the ground, was a jeep. Its driver, apparently asleep, sat motionless behind the wheel, his chin resting against his chest. Brent decided to go for the jeep.

Still concealed behind the door, he raised the right side of the robe and retrieved the Webley from its holster. He tucked his hands inside the sleeves of the black garment, pushed the door open with his hip, and walked down the stairs of the church. He was about five feet from the jeep when the driver's head came up and his eyes opened. Startled, the soldier reached instinctively for the automatic rifle propped on the seat next to him. But then, seeing that it was only the priest, he let his hand fall. Brent walked right up to him and murmured, "Forgive me, my son." Then he decked him with a gun butt to the side of the head.

As Brent pulled the slumped soldier out of the jeep and deposited him on the ground, another soldier came rushing out of the clinic, waving a pistol in the air and shouting in an aggrieved tone. Brent grabbed the weapon from the seat and ducked behind the jeep as a shot rang out. Pushing the hood of the robe off his head for better visibility, he sighted in on the approaching soldier and squeezed the trigger. The man fell in his tracks, raising a cloud of dust as he thudded against the ground.

Within seconds, soldiers came pouring through the door of the clinic. They pointed to their fallen comrade and looked around in all directions. One of them set the others straight, and they began to direct their fire at the jeep. Brent hugged the side of the jeep as bullets thudded into it and ricocheted in all directions. His heart sank as two loud pops and a sudden tilt told him that the tires on the passenger side had blown.

That ended all hopes of escaping in the jeep. As he

reached around it and fired back, Brent wondered how on earth he was going to capture the flatbed truck, which now appeared to be the only operative vehicle left in the village. He ducked lower as the jeep's windshield shattered noisily. It was hard to imagine how things could get worse.

Thirty seconds later, he knew. From overhead and behind him came the sound of a helicopter. He fired a few quick bursts in succession at the troops to keep them occupied, and then sneaked a quick glance back at the chopper. It was coming in low and fast, its bulbous nose honing right in on his position. He appeared to be right in the pilot's scope. He swung around toward the chopper and raised his weapon in a last-ditch effort to shoot it out of the sky. It might be a futile gesture, one man against a combat-equipped chopper, but he wasn't going out with a clip that wasn't empty.

But before Brent could squeeze off a single round, the deafening racket of heavy-caliber weaponry filled the air. Faster than he could throw himself to the ground, bullets whistled a few feet over his head, slammed into the flatbed truck, and reduced it to pieces of scrap metal.

He was still shielding his head when the chopper swooped down behind his position. The ferocious gusts from its blades enveloped him in a cloud of dust and almost beat him to the ground. Thoroughly puzzled, Brent turned to look at the chopper through protectively splayed fingers. Had that volley been a near miss with him as the intended target, or had they really meant to demolish the truck? Were they swooping down now to finish him off?

His confusion turned to astonishment as he recognized the figure in the open cargo door as Taamrat. Before Brent could acknowledge him, Taamrat leaped nimbly from the strut, the weapon in his hands chattering even as his boots thudded onto the ground. He laid down a blistering hail of fire, dropping some troops in their tracks and driving the rest to cover inside the clinic.

Recovering his wits, Brent jumped to his feet, tore off the black robe, and joined Taamrat in stitching the front of the building with round after round of fire. Taamrat jerked his head urgently over his shoulder, signaling Brent to enter the helicopter. Brent threw himself through the open cargo door and then reached back to pull Taamrat in after him.

As Taamrat flattened himself against the floor and assumed a firing position, Brent yelled to the pilot, "Take her behind the clinic! To the gully!"

The pilot nodded and skillfully took his craft straight up and over the clinic building in a tight arc before any of the soldiers below could so much as poke a head out the door. To make sure that the chopper remained unmolested, Taamrat leaned over and kept up a steady rain of covering fire.

Within seconds, the pilot shot over the building and swooped down to the edge of the gully. As the chopper hovered there, Brent leaped to the ground, reached down into the gully, and pulled a surprised Melissa out by her uplifted arms. With Brent supporting her, the two of them leaned against the gale created by the roaring blades and headed for the cargo door.

Brent grasped Melissa by the waist and raised her into Taamrat's waiting arms. As he piled headfirst into the chopper, Brent yelled, "Go!" The chopper leaped into the air, its stunning velocity pinning the three of them to the floor. When the force had eased and he could move again, Brent grabbed the handle and closed the hatch door. Finally, he turned toward Taamrat with an inquiring look and said, "So what kept you so long, dude?"

As Brent reached the outskirts of Addis Ababa, he slowed down the Rover and proceeded at a more relaxed pace. From the time that Taamrat had flown them back to their concealed Rover and then sped away to his headquarters, Melissa and Brent had spent a tense but uneventful journey. A ride in the helicopter would have been infinitely faster, of course, but it would have attracted unwanted attention.

Brent was headed for the airport. In a telephone call from a gas station along the way, Melissa had informed her friends at the college of recent events and asked for their advice. They were unhesitating in offering her help and a place to stay. But they were also candid in telling her that a wave of anticapitalist demonstrations had been sweeping the city for the last two days, disrupting services and making life a bit more uncomfortable for foreigners. Reluctantly, Melissa had found the advice of her friends, added to Brent's insistence that she temporarily leave the country, to be compelling.

As soon as he had dropped Melissa off at the airport and seen her flight take off, Brent was going to continue north to meet up with Taamrat again. They had more details to iron out about the aid agreements, and Brent wanted to check for himself, as discreetly as he could, on the loyalty of Taamrat's staff. Taamrat was sensitive about the issue, but sometimes a man could be blinded by old allegiances. Brent feared that something of the sort might be happening to Taamrat, and that the mole whom Brent was seeking might just be buried in Taamrat's own staff.

Melissa suddenly broke in on his reverie: "What's going on up ahead? I think that's a policeman." She placed a hand on his arm. "It looks like a roadblock of some kind."

Her tension communicated itself to Brent. She was right. Traffic was slowing down, and up ahead, a couple of policemen were stopping vehicles and talking to the drivers. Brent reached back behind his seat and snared the Webley. He raised himself slightly and eased the gun under his right thigh, where it would be hidden but instantly available. He didn't like this development one bit.

He looked in the rearview mirror. A long line of traffic had already formed behind them, and there was no way now to turn around quickly or unobtrusively. They would just have to tough it out. He reached over and squeezed Melissa's hand. "Don't worry," he said with more confidence than he felt. "Let me do the talking."

Melissa glanced at the gun that was barely visible to her and shook her head wanly. "Let's hope that talking is all that goes on."

Inch by inch they crept forward until theirs was the next car in line. They watched the policeman straighten up and direct the driver in front of them to turn right and continue down a side street. Then he waved the Rover forward. Brent rolled down his window and smiled.

"Hello, officer. Looks like something is going on up ahead. Has there been an accident or something?"

"No, no accident, sir. It is a demonstration. The workers have taken to the streets to protest exploitation. Power to the people! And may I ask where you are heading, sir?''

''We're on our way to the airport.''

''The airport. Ah, I'm afraid that you have a particular problem today. The airport has been closed. And, anyway, the streets ahead leading to the airport are impassable.'' He pointed to the side street. ''I will ask you to drive that way. If you follow the barricades, you will be able to continue around the closed-off areas. But as for the airport. . . .'' He shook his head with weary certainty. ''Surely not today. Now, if you will, please move on.''

Brent nodded his appreciation and turned down the street indicated. As he drove off, scrupulously observing the speed limit, he kept a watchful eye on the rearview mirror. The policeman had wasted no time in turning his attention to the next car in line. It all seemed authentic enough.

''What do you think?'' Melissa asked. ''What should we do now?''

''Well, we could continue north and out of the city, but I don't like the idea of you spending any more time in the countryside than you absolutely have to.'' He turned his head and looked at Melissa. ''You did say that your friends at the college had offered to help, right?''

''Yes, they did, and I think that they really meant it. In fact, Nenga—she's the head of the zoology department—offered to take me into her campus apartment for as long as I want. She's really sweet.''

''Is she married?''

''As a matter of fact, she's single, but why should that matter?''

''With an unmarried person, there won't be the complication of too many eyes and ears.'' He was silent for a moment. ''You know, that sounds like an acceptable option until these demonstrations peter out and the airport is back to normal. What do you think? How do you feel about staying with her?''

''I guess that I'd be comfortable with that arrangement. Since I'd rather not leave at all, I suppose this isn't such a bad compromise.''

''That's a good way to look at it.'' Brent snapped his fingers as a thought occurred to him. ''I just thought of someone who could keep an extra-special eye on you and help you get to the airport safely when the time is opportune.''

Melissa looked at him curiously. ''Who's that?''

''An old friend of yours who happens to have good connections. Halima Legassa.''

Melissa broke into a relieved smile. ''Of course! Halima!''

Feeling very satisfied about their arrangements, Brent began working his way through the nearly empty side streets in the direction of the college campus.

''No! No! No!'' Taamrat pounded his fist on the field desk in frustration after clicking off his two-way radio.

Brent looked at him expectantly for an explanation. Taamrat was not given to outbursts. The matter must be something extremely serious.

Taamrat turned to an aide and snapped, ''Get the word out to break camp immediately! Government troops are heading in this direction! They've been spotted about seventy kilometers southeast.'' He shook his head wearily and looked at Brent. "That's the second time this week. They seem to have an uncanny sense of where we are."

Brent pressed the issue. "That's what I've been talking about for the last half hour. It's more than coincidence."

Taamrat glowered at Brent. "Don't start that traitor-in-your-headquarters lecture again. I don't need to hear that right now."

"It's not a question of what you like or don't like anymore. You've got to deal with this realistically. Look, even before I arrived in Ethiopia, and before I met anyone here, there was a reception committee waiting for me at the airport in Aden. They killed the agent who was waiting for me and they tried to do the same to me. They knew about my mission in extremely fine detail."

"Did you think about suspecting your own people back in the States?"

"You bet I did—first thing. I set Headquarters on the case like a bulldog, and everyone cleared. And I'm not talking about any Mickey Mouse investigation, Tommy. This one rattled cages. So I'm saying, if it wasn't on my end, there's nowhere else to look except on *your* end."

Taamrat looked speculatively at his friend. "Tell me— don't you realize that what you're saying rubs off on me personally? I'm the one on this end who holds all the pieces, you know. All the information filters through me. So a charge against my staff is tantamount to a charge against me."

It was finally out in the open. What was bothering Taamrat and what was bothering Brent were one and the same thing. Brent's worst nightmare had been that Taamrat, like the friend in Colombia who had set Brent up, had inexplicably turned traitor. He had hardly dared to admit it to himself, let alone say it out loud.

Brent met Taamrat's steely gaze. "I'll be honest with you," he said. "I did consider it. For about two minutes. But I think you know that I wouldn't hesitate to consider my own mother, if just to clear her once and for all. No, I know it's not you, Tommy. But I do think that someone on your end is taking advantage of you. Even if that strikes you as outrageous, it's not the same thing as pointing the finger at you, and I don't think of it that way."

Taamrat nodded appreciatively. "Fair enough. That clears the air, even if it still isn't very complimentary to me. And you're right. I have been sensitive about the possibility of a traitor in my own back pocket. So I'm inviting you to take a look around. Consider anybody and everybody, with no exceptions. You've got carte blanche."

"Thanks, Tommy. I know that it's not easy for you to say that." He placed his hand on Taamrat's shoulder. "Now it's time to think about ditching this place."

The chopper settled down with a slight bump and came to rest on the rocky plateau. As Brent and Taamrat stepped out, they were greeted by the sights and sounds of the hectic activity that always accompanies the setting up of a new bivouac. No sooner were tents raised and staked than supplies were being removed from trucks and carried inside by a constantly moving line of cursing and sweating troops. It always reminded Brent of an anthill.

Brent and Taamrat had just returned from a scouting mission. Taamrat made a fetish of keeping one step ahead of his government pursuers, and in practice, this meant staking out his next headquarters even before the last one had to be abandoned. Because of its importance, Taamrat insisted on personally supervising the operation.

Taamrat held the tent flap aside for Brent to enter. Brent started to step through, then stopped cold. "Nuts! I forgot my briefcase, T. I'm going to go back and retrieve it. Go on in and I'll join you in a couple of minutes."

"Sure. They say that the memory is the second thing to go, you know. Have you thought about cuffing that bag to your wrist?"

"Funny, funny."

Brent turned and retraced his steps. The sun was slipping over the rim of the western horizon, leaving gold and orange streaks across the sky like a gigantic finger painting. He paused to admire it, then resumed his trek to the helicopter. As he drew near, he caught sight of the pilot looking back at him through the cockpit window. From what Brent could see, he was casually replacing the radio handset on its holder. The pilot swung open his door invitationally, but Brent declined entry.

"Sorry," he said. "I forgot my briefcase. I'd forget my head if it wasn't screwed on. Would you mind handing it out to me?"

As Brent rested his hand against the side of the door, the pilot leaned over to his right and picked the briefcase off the floor. He made a show of dusting it off, then handed it over to Brent.

"Thank you much. See you later in the mess, right? I'm sure it'll be another gourmet delight."

The pilot laughed gruffly and turned back to the work of shutting down all the switches and putting the chopper to rest until its next use. Brent grasped the briefcase by its handle and walked away, whistling an old tune.

He was beginning to see the light. The invisible man— that's what the pilot was. Unassuming, always hovering in the background, always privy to what was going on. Overhearing all and saying next to nothing. Taamrat's chauffer, as it were, permanently within earshot in the driver's seat at all the critical moments. By the very nature of his job, he was a man who had to be kept up-to-date on all schedules and movements. There was probably nothing that escaped his notice, and it was all legitimate.

Brent looked at the briefcase. No traces of dye, so it hadn't been forced open. But he had left the briefcase in the back on the passenger bench, not on the floor right next to the pilot. To be fair, perhaps the pilot had noticed it and picked it up, intending to bring it to Brent later. But that wouldn't explain the faint scratches on the shiny surface of the lock, scratches that weren't there during the flight.

Brent slipped around an outcrop of rock and began to double back toward the helicopter through a shallow ravine. He hugged the shadows and stayed low, but he suspected that the pilot would be too busy to notice. He was right. The man was speaking in a low tone and in a foreign language, but his intensity and volubility left no doubt that he was feeding someone a lot of information in a short amount of time. The man could talk after all.

Brent got down on the ground and began to crawl closer to the craft. He came up under the passenger door and strained to listen. While he didn't know the language, perhaps he could glean something useful before putting the crunch on the pilot.

Now the pilot's voice fell silent, and the radio crackled in response. Brent cocked his ear. He heard the same unintelligible cadences. No way of deciphering all that. But as he listened, a certainty began to grow in his mind. He had heard that voice before. He definitely knew that voice. There was no question. But he didn't want to acknowledge it. The consequences were too painful. It was the voice of Halima Legassa.

Chapter Ten

Brent lay there for a few moments, immobilized by the realization that had crashed down upon him. The pilot was reporting to Halima Legassa. That made her an agent for the other side. And Melissa was in her hands. Brent felt a surge of anger and of fear that nauseated him. When it passed, he decided grimly that he had better start interrogating the pilot.

Even as the thought occurred to Brent, the pilot opened his door and began to step down. Peering beneath the undercarriage of the helicopter, Brent saw the pilot's right foot reach down and plant itself firmly on the ground. But then the pilot seemed to get hung up, as if his left foot had caught on something, and he stood there poised on one foot, frozen in place.

And then a voice rang out, cold with accusation and righteous indignation. Brent couldn't understand the words, but he recognized Taamrat's voice speaking in his own language to the pilot. Brent didn't need a translator to understand the venom and the raw hatred that the words imparted. There was death in that tone.

Brent scrambled to his feet and headed around the

helicopter. As Brent raced around the front end, Taamrat had already reached the pilot and thrown him violently against the side of the helicopter. He smashed a left fist into the pilot's kidney and followed it with a right cross to the face. The pilot crumpled to the ground like a rag doll. Taamrat had pulled his foot back to aim a heavy boot at the pilot's head when Brent reached him. He wrapped his arms around Taamrat's chest, pinned his arms to his side, and pushed him away from the pilot. Taamrat's eyes flashed irrationally, and his chest heaved as if it would burst.

"Cool it," Brent said. "It's okay. We've got him now. It's all right."

Gradually, he was able to calm Taamrat down and restore his self-control. He knew that if he had not been there to stop him, Taamrat would have killed the pilot with his bare hands. Brent could understand the betrayal of trust that could temporarily turn a man into a raging animal. Finally, he was able to release Taamrat. They stood there looking down at the unconscious man sprawled at their feet.

Taamrat pointed at him contemptuously. "I'll never be able to understand how that slime could have done it. How could he betray his own people? How could he turn on me after all that we've been through together? I've saved his bacon and he's saved mine I don't know how many times."

"There's probably an answer, but I bet that it won't mean much to either one of us, Tommy. We're just on a totally different wavelength, I guess. Guys like him will never make sense to people who believe in loyalty and friendship."

Taamrat turned to Brent, compassion in his gaze. "I don't exactly know how to tell you this, but from what I overheard when I was standing there. . . ."

"I know—Melissa's in trouble. I recognized the person he was talking to. Did you get any details at all?"

"Just where she is right now, but they're planning to move her to another location in the morning. We'd better get our act together and move out now. Let's get this crud back to camp and grab some help, including my backup pilot."

Brent felt a burst of warmth and gratitude. Not a moment's hesitation in Taamrat's offer. Not the shadow of a doubt that Brent's problem was automatically *his* problem. "Thanks, guy," Brent murmured in a gruff tone that said it all.

After the helicopter had landed in the darkened soccer stadium at the outskirts of the city, five shadowy figures slipped out and scaled the chain-link fence that surrounded the grassy field. They dropped silently to the ground and moved cautiously toward the nearby highway.

They crouched in some bushes adjacent to the gravel shoulder of the road until they heard the sound of an approaching truck. Then one of the figures detached himself from the others and ran out onto the asphalt surface. As the truck's headlights picked him out and illuminated him, he stumbled a few times and then fell flat on his back in the middle of the road. The driver applied his brakes in a panic and the furniture truck came to a squealing stop just inches from the inert form.

The driver jumped from his cab and ran forward toward the man he was sure he had just killed. As he bent over the body, a hand shot out and grabbed his arm. "Thank you, comrade, for the use of your truck. No resistance, no noise, no problem—right?" Taamrat nailed the shaken man with his unwavering gaze.

"Oh, yes, comrade. No problem. It's yours. Power to the people," he concluded in a weak voice.

"Good man." Taamrat couldn't resist a little playfulness. "Can we drop you off somewhere?"

"Oh, no! No! I'll just start walking." He turned a worried look upon Taamrat's unsmiling face. "With your permission, of course."

"Start walking, brother."

With a smile on his face, Taamrat turned and ran to the driver's side of the truck. He hoisted himself up and slid behind the wheel. Brent was already seated on the passenger side. The other three men were in place in the back, wedged in among various pieces of furniture.

Taamrat depressed the clutch and shifted into first. "Hang on, boys and girls! We're on our way."

Thirteen minutes later they were pulling to the curb on a side street flanking the Ministry of Justice. It was a looming brick building that housed administrative offices and courtrooms. More to their purpose, it also housed cells in its cavernous basement.

Taamrat cut the engine and they sat there for a moment on the dark and deserted street, studying the lay of the land. The basement windows were all secured with formidable metal bars. Ditto for the first floor. Above that level, the casement windows were closed but more vulnerable to entry. Of the two dozen or so windows that were visible, lights shone from behind only four, and three of those were on the basement level.

Brent looked around for any signs of activity on the street. "Why not pull up on the sidewalk next to the building? Let's go in through the second floor."

Taamrat nodded. "That's the way I read it too. Hang on, men." He started the engine, turned the wheel, and backed the truck up slowly until its right rear tire bumped up onto the sidewalk, tilting the truck dangerously. Another bump for the left rear tire, and then he backed up slowly until the tailgate just brushed against the building. He cut the engine again, leaving the front tires resting on the street.

All five men scrambled out the front doors and assisted each other to the roof of the truck. Brent hoisted himself up on the shoulders of two of the men and reached for the ledge of a second-story window. He grasped the gritty cement with his fingers and pulled himself up, the toes of his boots finding slender purchase in the grooves between the bricks. When he had lifted himself on straining arms to the level of his waist, he raised one knee and placed it on the cement ledge. After lifting his hands and pushing against the bricks on either side of the window frame for leverage, he pulled up the other knee until he was kneeling on the ledge with the side of his face pressed against the cool glass.

He turned his head slightly to peer into the room. By the light entering the room from the hallway transom, he could make out some desks and file cabinets. There were no lights on in the room itself, and it appeared to be empty. Brent turned and directed an elbow at the top pane of glass. With one swift blow he shattered the glass, and then he reached through the gaping hole and opened the window lock on the sash.

He pushed the top edge of the lower window frame up an inch from the outside with the tips of his fingers. Then he reached down under the window and shoved it all the way up. Bending down, he slid through the open window and dropped to the floor. Next, he reached back out and grasped Taamrat's wrist as he was hoisted up by two men. When four of them had climbed up and entered the room, the fifth man jumped down from the roof of the truck and slid behind the wheel, watchful and ready.

Wordlessly, the men crept to the door. Brent eased it open and listened. Nothing. He stuck his head out and looked down the corridor in both directions. Again, nothing. He signaled to the others, and one by one they slipped out of the room and down the corridor, weapons at the ready.

They came to the central portion of the hallway. To their left, two open cage elevator shafts stood side by side. Across from the elevators was the door leading to a staircase. Voices drifted up from below through the elevator shafts. They sounded calm and normal. Then a door slammed and all was silent.

Taamrat turned to one of his men and spoke in a low voice: "Give us exactly sixty seconds. Then press both elevator buttons and bring them up to this level. Stay here and secure this corridor."

Brent, Taamrat, and the remaining man entered the stairwell. Brent sat on the railing and slid sideways down to the next landing, where he repeated the process. The other two followed suit. It allowed for a swift descent and eliminated the sound of footsteps. When they reached the doorway outside the basement level, they clustered around Taamrat, watching the second hand of his watch sweep toward its mark. Just as Taamrat said "Go!" the elevator motors sprang into action on the other side of the door. Brent flung the corridor door open and sprinted toward the right. Taamrat turned left and raced that way. The third man stationed himself at the stairway door.

Just as Brent pulled up even with a door on his right, it opened unexpectedly to reveal a soldier with a puzzled look on his face. Brent struck him with the butt of his rifle and the soldier carried that look to the floor. Brent stepped over the inert form and entered the room from which the man had emerged.

It was a locker room, and seated on a wooden bench, tying the lace of a boot, was a shirtless man in khaki trousers. Brent laid him low before he had a chance to open his mouth. From the room beyond came the sound of running water. Brent flattened himself against the wall next to the door. Then he poked his head in quickly and pulled back. It was a shower room. A fat soldier was lathering his hair under a stream of steaming water as he whistled out of tune.

Brent cupped his hand over his mouth and hollered, "Yo! Out here!" The words reverberated from the cinder-block walls, causing a hollow echo. The shower stopped and Brent heard wet feet plodding across the cement floor. When the man emerged angrily from the shower room with a towel around his waist and his hair still foaming with lather, Brent jammed the barrel of the gun into his rib cage and prodded him over to an open locker. Brent motioned the incredulous man to get in, and somehow he managed to squeeze his bulk inside the cramped space of the locker. Brent slammed the door, turned the key in the lock, pulled it out, and threw it over the tops of the lockers. It landed behind them, bounced with a clink, and came to rest out of sight.

That accounted for everyone in here. Brent went back to the corridor, prepared to continue searching toward the right, but he caught the frantic signal of his colleague guarding the stairwell. Brent ran to him on the double. "What's up?" he asked.

"Taamrat. He is five doorways down. He said come when you can."

Brent rushed down the corridor on light feet. When he had counted off five doors, he pressed his back against the wall and stood there for a moment, straining to listen. Suddenly, a shot rang out, then another. Brent flung the door open and threw himself in, landing on his stomach.

The soldier standing with his back to him turned in time to squeeze off a shot, but he was aiming chest high and Brent was on the floor. Brent fired from his prone position and the soldier spun to the right and dropped to the floor, landing on his own weapon.

A shot ricocheted off the floor scant inches from Brent's face, and he rolled quickly to his left and behind a desk, pursued by more shots. He rose to a crouching position, took a deep breath, and reached back around the edge of the desk.

His attacker was crouched behind the base of a water cooler. Brent took aim at the upturned bottle of water and fired. The bottle shattered explosively, spraying water and shards of glass in all directions. The crouching soldier yelped in pain as a chunk of flying glass pierced his forehead. As he reacted, he exposed half his torso from behind the cooler. Brent got off a clean shot and the man toppled to the floor.

From behind him, out in the corridor, Brent heard the echoing sounds of a firefight. The man guarding the stairwell was holding his position, but there was no telling for how long. Brent looked around. At the back end of this room was a metal door. It merited investigation. That's where Taamrat had to be.

Brent ran to the door and opened it just a crack. Ominous silence. He pulled it open carefully, willing the door not to squeak. Then he poked one eye around the corner of the door. This was the lockup. Cells lined both sides of this corridor. He thought he could make out several figures huddled at the back of their cells at the far end of the corridor. He would have expected them to be right up front, grasping the bars, curious about the sounds all around them. It just didn't feel right.

Suddenly, a figure jumped out from one of the cells, crouching and firing. Brent ducked back as several bullets pounded into the doorframe where his head had just been. Accurate but slow. He knelt, shifted the gun to his left hand, and sprayed a few bursts around the corner at ankle level. As he sqeezed off the third burst, he rolled over and into the corridor. When the soldier leaped out of the cell again to fire in his direction, Brent released a volley that cut him down. The man toppled face down into the corridor outside the cell.

Crawling sinuously with a paddling motion imparted by knees and elbows, Brent worked his way down the corridor toward the fallen soldier, all his senses alert. When he reached the body and saw what was in the cell, he pushed the dead man aside and detoured into the cell.

Taamrat was lying on his back, blood oozing from a wicked crease across the left side of his forehead. With his heart in his throat, Brent checked for a pulse. As he touched the side of Taamrat's neck, Taamrat groaned and moved his head slowly from side to side. He was alive but needed medical attention. Unfortunately, that would have to wait just a little longer.

Brent rose to his feet and walked slowly out of the cell. He turned right and moved inexorably down the corridor. At the back wall, in the last two cells, he could make out three figures. As he drew closer on slightly bent knees, with his rifle extended and sweeping from side to side, he could identify the three people with absolute certainty, even in the inadequate light provided by the dim bulbs. As he drew within a few yards, all three figures moved deliberately out of the facing cells and into the center of the corridor, their backs literally to the wall.

In unwavering hands, Halima Legassa held a weapon pointed right at Brent's head. Yämärgän, his head swathed in bandages, held Melissa in front of him, her eyes wild with fear, a gleaming knife pressed against her throat. He crouched behind her, almost comically trying to use her slender body as a shield. Although entire portions of his body were exposed, he was managing to protect his vital centers. Brent could not be certain of a clean and killing shot.

"You have caused me much trouble, Mr. Collins," Legassa said. "I am glad to see it come to an end."

Brent shifted the barrel of his gun in her direction. "I'm afraid it's a draw, Legassa. Why don't you drop your gun? Then we'll talk. Maybe we can strike a bargain."

"You fool! Do you think you can walk in here and

then just walk out again? You'll never get away! You're surrounded.''

"Oh, I don't know. It's working out in my favor so far. I think you'll find that your garrison has shrunk considerably. In fact, unless I'm mistaken, you two may be on your own.''

For a second, a worried look played over her face. It was quickly replaced with contempt and fury. "How dare you interfere in the workings of the glorious revolution! Who do you Americans think you are that you can push us around and oppose the will of the people? You make me sick! I will not rest until your miserable country has been beaten into submission and oblivion! Until all capitalist pigs are dead! Dead!''

She was practically sputtering, and that had Brent worried. She had the sound of a true believer, a zealot who didn't always recognize reality or act in her own best interest. Her voice now had the frenzied quality of those terrorists who blow themselves up to make a point intelligible only to their own twisted minds.

Brent raised his left hand placatingly. "All right, now. Don't get excited. Just let Melissa go and we'll work everything out. She hasn't done anything to you. Let her go."

Legassa burst out into mirthless, hysterical laughter. "Let Melissa go? Let her go, did you say? Let her die, you mean! And die yourself! Let all pigs die!''

She turned toward Yämärgän, who had been listening impassively, and she shrieked at him, "Kill the girl! Kill her! Slice her throat!''

Horrified, Brent watched animation suddenly flow into Yämärgän's eyes and a smile begin to crease his face.

The pink tip of his tongue dreamily licked his lips and then withdrew.

As Melissa opened her mouth in a wordless scream, Brent was faced with an impossible decision. If he managed to make a one-in-a-million shot and hit one of Yämärgän's vital centers, Halima Legassa would drop him with an easy shot and then kill Melissa herself. If he shot Legassa, Melissa's throat would be slit open before he could swing around and drop her killer.

All this raced through his mind in seconds as his hands and eyes and brain instinctively reacted. Without conscious thought, his weapon turned unerringly toward Yämärgän, and his finger squeezed the trigger. The bullet penetrated Yämärgän's right shoulder, causing a fine red mist to spray on the whitewashed wall immediately behind him. As he dropped heavily to the floor, the knife fell harmlessly from his slack fingers, clattered against the tiles, and slid into a cell.

Simultaneously, Brent heard Melissa's piercing scream and the reverberating explosion of another weapon firing. He flinched involuntarily, already expecting the bite of cold steel through his flesh and sinews and muscles, already waiting for the descent of darkness and the silence that never ends.

But he found himself still standing. It was Halima Legassa who slumped to the floor, curses still frothing on her twisted lips. Brent turned around slowly, still in a daze. Taamrat leaned against the bars of his cell, a pistol dangling from his fingers. As Brent opened his arms wide and gathered Melissa into them, his eyes grew blurry. But he managed to control his voice as he issued a mock complaint over his shoulder: "Hey, dude, what kept you so long?"

Taamrat smiled weakly, slumped slowly to the floor, and passed out. Brent and Melissa ran to him. They checked his pulse and then tore a strip of cloth from his shirt for a bandage. No time to waste. Brent placed the automatic weapon in Melissa's hands. Then he lifted Taamrat from the floor of the cell and transferred his limp body to his shoulders in a fireman's carry. As he and Melissa emerged from the cell and turned left to go back to the main corridor, Brent glanced back to the right. Halima Legassa's body lay sprawled on the green tile floor. But Yämärgän was nowhere in sight.

Chapter Eleven

As dawn broke two days later, Brent and Melissa, accompanied by three heavily armed rebel soldiers, stepped warily from the hatch door of a helicopter at the edge of Melissa's devastated camp. The furtive visit was the result of a compromise. Mindful of the danger, Brent had reluctantly agreed that Melissa could spend an hour or so checking on the condition of the jackals and retrieving whatever records could be found intact. In return, Melissa had agreed to fly back immediately to the States until things had cooled down and it was safe for her to resume her fieldwork.

Yesterday, before working out the compromise with Melissa, Brent had arranged to have Taamrat transported to an American carrier plying the Red Sea. The carrier had state-of-the-art medical facilities that rivaled anything available in a land-based hospital. At last report, Taamrat had been taken off the critical list and reported to be on his way to recovery.

Now Brent and Melissa, their flanks protected by two soldiers whose suspicious eyes constantly swept the surrounding area, approached the base camp that vindictive government troops had pillaged earlier that week. The three flattened tents still lay sprawled on the ground like some giant's discarded clothes. Off to one side, Melissa's burned-out Blazer had long since stopped smoldering, but its sooty and blistered finish still suggested hot metal. All in all, the camp looked desolate and unappealing. Brent was sure that Melissa was just as anxious as he to gather up what was salvageable and get away from the depressing atmosphere.

Melissa gestured toward one of the crumpled tents. "That's where I'd like to start," she said. "I kept my records there. Do you think we could prop it up so I can go inside?"

Brent and one of the soldiers set to work raising the telescoping poles, and within a few minutes the tent was standing again, although it had acquired a pronounced tilt to the right. Melissa entered the tent, shook her head at the mess before her, and grimly set to work gathering up notebooks and loose sheets of paper. The soldier went back outside to join his vigilant companion, but Brent stayed with Melissa, dutifully following her around with a wooden crate into which she placed what she needed to save.

Melissa dropped another looseleaf binder into the crate and then sat back on her haunches.

"This is so depressing! I spent the better part of two years gathering this information, and those soldiers trashed it in just two minutes."

"I know, Melissa. It's enough to frost me too, and I haven't even put any time into this project. But at least they didn't burn your papers. They're all messed up, but they're intact. You'll get it all back together again. Believe me, it looks worse than it is.''

Melissa smiled at him gratefully. ''You're right, of course. The glass is half full. And I will have plenty of time to rearrange the data and begin to draw conclusions when I'm back in the States.''

''With some time left over for me, I hope.''

Melissa reached for his hand, a twinkle in her eye. ''Oh, I think that can be arranged.''

Brent leaned toward her and kissed her. His heart was light. Melissa represented a new and wonderful chapter in his life, and his assignment here in Ethiopia was about to come to a successful conclusion. And when Taamrat was back on his feet and able to command his newly equipped forces, Brent was certain that this poor, tortured country would be entering a new and better chapter in its history too. Reluctantly, Brent released Melissa's hand. ''We'd better finish up here and be on our way. It's not a great place to linger.''

They were working on their third boxload when the stillness outside was shattered by bursts from automatic weapons. Brent dropped the crate and pulled Melissa to the floor of the tent, urging her to stay flat. Shouts now filled the air, and the sounds of a full-fledged firefight rose in volume. Brent grabbed his AR–15, crawled swiftly to the entrance flap, and looked out.

From here he had a clear view of the charred shell of Melissa's car. Two of the rebel soldiers were crouched behind the Blazer for cover, and they were directing a steady barrage of fire at a stand of trees about two hundred yards away. The helicopter pilot was doing the same from beneath the chopper. All signs pointed unmistakably to an ambush.

Brent crawled back to Melissa. He removed his Webley from its holster and held it out to her. ''Here, use this if you have to. The safety is off. All you have to do is squeeze the trigger. And aim for the chest, not the head.'' Gingerly, Melissa accepted the weapon.

Brent reached for the rope handle of the crate he had dropped and dragged it over next to Melissa. Then he moved the other two crates to form a triangular shield around her. It wasn't much, but it was certainly better than nylon tent fabric for stopping stray or intentional bullets.

Satisfied that Melissa now had at least a modicum of protection, Brent crawled to the back end of the tent. He raised his head to the level of a wedge-shaped tear in the back wall of the tent and peered out. He could see clumps of brush and vegetation—the very cover, in fact, where Melissa had hidden from government troops only days before.

He pulled his hunting knife from its scabbard and slashed a low horizontal opening through the nylon fabric. Returning the knife to its holder, he paused long enough to blow a kiss to Melissa, and then he rolled through the gash onto the ground outside. Rising to his feet but crouching low, he made a dash for cover. He reached the brush without incident and dived into it. Sitting up, he gestured to his wary comrades in arms, whose peripheral vision had registered his motion, to let them know his new position. They acknowledged him with a wave of the hand and turned back to business.

Brent crouched in the brush for a few minutes, assessing the situation. The tent blocked his view of the clump of trees, but his trained ear told him that three separate weapons were being fired from that direction. A careful visual sweep soon convinced him that the ambush was confined to one sector, the direction toward which Taamrat's troops were firing. That was good news. At least they were not surrounded or hopelessly outnumbered. This must be one of the small patrols that had been scouring the countryside in recent weeks in an attempt to restrict nomadic migrations. Their arrival was bad luck, but it was a salvageable situation.

Suddenly, Brent heard a rustling sound in the brush just a few yards away. He swung the barrel of his weapon in that direction, finger already tightening on the trigger. He stayed his finger at the last second as a long, slender muzzle topped by quizzically pointed ears suddenly popped into view. Brent broke into a grin. Leave it to old Starback to join the fray. He reached out a hand to pet him, but the jackal backed away and disappeared into the undergrowth. Obviously, domestication was not high on his list of behavior patterns.

After another minute of deliberation, Brent decided to circle around behind the enemy position. Since the tent was shielding him, he had every reason to believe that the attackers were unaware of his presence. If he could work his way around behind them, they would be caught in a crossfire. Brent picked up a stone and lobbed it toward the two men behind the Blazer. It bounced next to one of the kneeling soldiers, and he turned toward Brent. Brent pointed to himself, then indicated with his hands what he was about to do. The soldier nodded vigorously, endorsing the plan and signaling his understanding.

Brent turned and forced his way through the brush and brambles away from the tent and the clump of trees. When he emerged on the other side, he found that the ground sloped down toward a gully before it rose again and extended toward the horizon in an unbroken plain. Brent scrambled down into the gully and followed it to the right. When he had gone about thirty yards, he came to an intersecting dry-bed channel. Cutting right again, he crouched below the lip of the channel and headed toward the sound of gunfire. When it seemed to be loudest, he stopped.

Cautiously, he raised himself just high enough so that he could peek over the top of the channel. Sure enough, three government soldiers were sheltered behind a grove of trees, and they were directing sporadic fire at the Blazer a couple of hundred yards away. One of them had paused to reload. Now was a good time to make a move.

Brent rose to his full height, aimed just above the heads of the soldiers, and directed a few bursts into the trunks of the trees. All three jumped to their feet and turned toward Brent simultaneously, stunned looks on their faces. "Throw down your weapons—now!" Brent ordered. All three men just stood there, frozen into immobility. Brent directed another burst of gunfire into the trees. Startled, two of the soldiers complied at once, flinging their weapons to the ground and raising their hands high above their heads. The third man looked uncertainly at his companions, started to raise the barrel of his weapon in Brent's direction, but then had second thoughts. Brent nodded approvingly as he, too, dropped his weapon to the ground and reached for the sky.

Brent shouted to his companions, and soon all three

of them were heading toward his position on the double. They frisked the captured soldiers for other weapons as Brent covered them. Then the rebel troops had one of the prisoners hug a tree while they secured his wrists on the other side of the tree with his own belt. They followed suit with the other two captured soldiers. This would keep the prisoners out of the way until Brent and his party were ready to move out.

Satisfied, Brent grinned at his comrades and said, "Good job. No lives lost, nobody hurt, and three squirming fish in the net. Not bad for one day's work." The men laughed and slapped one another on the back in congratulations. Brent left them, still flushed with victory, and headed for the tent to check on Melissa's safety. As he drew anxiously near, he was relieved beyond words to see her emerge from the tent.

He raised a hand in reassurance. "It's okay," he called out. "Everything's wrapped up and nobody got hurt. What about. . . ." He stopped in midsentence. There was something about Melissa's posture that made him alert suddenly. It looked too tense, too stiff. Melissa walked about three feet from the tent, turned to face Brent, and then stopped. Brent could now see the stricken look on her face. Something was terribly wrong. And then Yämärgän drew aside the tent flap and stepped out into the sunlight.

If it had not been for the Webley in his hand, Yämärgän probably would have inspired snickers. His head and his right shoulder were swathed in oversized bandages. One forlorn ear stuck out like a becalmed sail. The other lay hidden, flattened uselessly against his head by its surgical coverings. He looked like a roly-poly mummy beginning to emerge from its wrappings. But the pistol aimed at Melissa killed any impulse Brent might have had to laugh.

"Come back over here, my little dove." The insistent rumble of Yämärgän's voice was accompanied by a nod indicating the area behind the tent. With fear written on her face, Melissa turned and walked reluctantly to where he had indicated. Yämärgän reached out and seized her arm with his pudgy fingers as she walked past him. Brent flinched at the sight. "And you, Señor Macho, put down the rifle. Slowly. Carefully. *Bueno*. Now come over here with us."

As Brent placed the weapon on the ground and moved toward Yämärgän, he prayed fervently that Taamrat's troops would notice that something was amiss. But there was no outcry or disturbance behind him. They were probably still celebrating their bloodless victory and exulting over their prisoners. They would have no reason now to cover Brent or to note his progress.

As Brent drew closer, Yämärgän backed slowly away with Melissa at his side, each step taking his bulk farther behind the tent and out of sight of the soldiers. His right hand still imprisoned Melissa's arm, and his left hand, resting on the overstuffed shelf of his stomach, still directed the Webley at her heart.

"Yes. This is far enough." Yämärgän gestured at Brent with the gun. "We have a score to settle, as you Yankees say." He touched his bandaged head with his right hand, then pointed to his shoulder with the gun. "This is your work, no? You have caused this to be done to Yämärgän, no? And so it deserves a response." His arm shot out again to grasp Melissa, who had begun edging away from him. "No, no, my lovely, you must stay and see this. You must, in fact, help me in this."

Melissa began to squirm in his grasp. Involuntarily, Brent took a step forward. Instantly, Yämärgän's arm shot up and directed the barrel of the gun at Brent's chest. "No! No motion from you!" For the first time, desperation had crept into his voice. Yämärgän pulled Melissa to him roughly and wrapped his arm around her neck. He nuzzled the Webley against her temple. "Any more tricks from you and she will die! I swear this!"

Brent watched helplessly as Melissa continued to struggle and to suddenly squeal in Yämärgän's grasp. He was stymied. If it had been just Yämärgän and himself, he would have made a move right this instant. The longer that the standoff continued, Brent knew, the more the odds tilted in Yämärgän's favor. Swift, decisive, and deadly action was called for. But as long as Melissa was vulnerable and in harm's way, nothing could be done.

As Yämärgän grew more exasperated with Melissa's squirmings and her high-pitched squeals, he began to shake her from side to side like a rag doll. Brent was being pushed beyond his limits. He made a fist, tensed his leg muscles, and prepared to push off.

And then, streaking like a flash of lightning from the underbrush, Starback suddenly raced across the intervening distance and launched himself into the air. He landed on Yämärgän's shoulder with an impact that caused even that huge man to stumble sideways. Unerringly, the jackal's razor-sharp fangs sought out Yämärgän's ear, clamped around it, and sank in viciously. Screaming in pain and in terror, Yämärgän dropped the gun and fell heavily to the ground. His hands flailed at the snarling jackal in an unsuccessful attempt to dislodge him.

Before a startled Brent could move, Melissa picked up the gun and pointed it straight at Yämärgän's upturned face. "Don't you dare hurt that animal! Do you hear me? Stop that! Right now!"

To Brent's amazement, Yämärgän dropped his hands helplessly and began to whimper. Starback, his teeth still clamped around his prize, looked sideways at Melissa. She said, "It's okay, Starback. Good boy! You can let go now." The jackal eased his jaws open and backed off, his eyes never leaving Yämärgän. He growled once more for good measure, and Yämärgän trembled with renewed fear.

Brent turned as the three soldiers came pounding around the corner of the tent. They stared unbelievingly at the sight that met their eyes. Brent told them, "It's okay, guys. Melissa's just doing a little mopping up operation here. One more fish for the net." He looked down contemptuously at Yämärgän. "No, better make that a whale."

Epilogue

Washington, D.C.
April 16

Dear Taamrat,

I've been following your exploits on the evening news as you work your way toward Addis Ababa. What the newscasters don't know would fill a month's worth of Sunday specials, but I must say that you are getting dynamite press. They keep showing clips of you in your designer fatigues and referring to you as a matinee idol. Jane Pauley looks like she's drooling over you. Give me a break, will you?

By now, you must have broken in all the toys that our uncle sent you for your birthday. Otherwise, you'd still be holed up in your cabin in the woods, dreaming of future days of glory. Be sure to shoot a few varmints for me. It looks like I'll be kicking around this corner of the world for a while. I sure would like to join you for a safari, but I know that I'd have an impossible time getting a visa. I seem to have become persona non grata in your neck of the woods because of an unfortunate barroom

185

brawl. I guess I'll just have to wait until a friendlier government takes over.

Listen, T, the reason I'm writing you is to ask you a favor. Melissa and I would like to invite you to a wedding—our wedding. In fact, she wants you to be best man. I told her that Woody Allen had asked for first crack, but she seems to have her heart set on you. How about it? Think that you can pull yourself away from your diversions for a quick weekend? If not, we'll certainly understand, and we'll find a proxy. You're to be the official witness of record no matter what. That's what the boss says. By the way, the date is set for June 15. How about that? I'm going to be a June groom.

I'm going to send this through our courier service. The post office can't seem to keep a current address on you. You've got to start paying the rent.

Take care, dude.

Your buddy,
Brent

DATE DUE

MAY 13 '91	JAN 06 94	
MAY 27 '91	MAR 01 '94	
JUN 11 '91	OCT 09 '98	
JUL 29 '91	FEB 1 9 '99	
SEP 0 3 '91	FEB 1 9 1900	
OCT 0 1 '91		
DEC 0 3 1991		
AUG 0 8 1992		
JAN 2 8 '93		
AUG 0 6 '93		
SEP 0 9 '93		